To I

MW01491225

BLIND DATE WITH
THE HERO

HEROES OF FREEDOM RIDGE

TARA GRACE ERICSON

merry Christmas!

Tara Grace Ericson

Published in the United States of America
Cover Designer: Amanda Walker PA & Design Services
Editor: Editing Done Write
Ebook ISBN: 978-1-949896-43-5
Paperback ISBN: 978-1-949896-44-2

CONTENTS

Chapter 1	1
Chapter 2	12
Chapter 3	26
Chapter 4	39
Chapter 5	48
Chapter 6	58
Chapter 7	69
Chapter 8	78
Chapter 9	100
Chapter 10	111
Chapter 11	121
Chapter 12	125
Chapter 13	137
Chapter 14	154
Chapter 15	168
Chapter 16	175
Epilogue	186
Acknowledgments	191
Other Books in the Heroes of Freedom Ridge Series	193
Books by Tara Grace Ericson	195
About the Author	197

To my fellow Freedom Ridge authors, for taking a chance on this project and being an absolute joy to work with. And to the readers of Freedom Ridge, who have embraced this series so completely. I'd buy you all a cup of coffee at Stories and Scones if I could.

"The Lord turns my darkness into light."

— 2 SAMUEL 22:29

1

---

*A*lexis glanced up at her opponent through her tears, swiping at the sweat beading on her brow. Her lips felt like she'd kissed the scorching lava flows she'd once seen in Guatemala.

"Give up, Alexis."

She narrowed her eyes at Toby.

"Never," she replied firmly. The word came out jumbled and unclear, since her tongue felt like a brick in her mouth. Her stomach roiled in protest as she picked up another hot wing.

"Face it, cher. Your California soul can't hang with my Cajun roots."

Alexis glared at him, despite the Cajun term of endearment he pronounced as "shaw". As much as she hated to admit it, she was afraid he was right.

She was only three wings into the so-called Denver Diablo Challenge. Her sinuses would be clear all season from the heat.

"I missed it. What did she bet this time?"

The question came from Tessa, who was at the other end of the table, next to Adam, her husband. They both worked at Got Your Six Security. Just like everyone else at the table here to witness her embarrassment.

Alexis desperately wanted to wipe her nose, but the rubber gloves made it impossible. She watched helplessly as Toby pulled another clean bone neatly out of his mouth. He only had one more.

"Alexis agreed to go on ten blind dates before New Year's Eve."

Heath, her boss. She didn't appreciate the bit of laughter in his tone.

"She what?" Tessa's exclamation of disbelief turned heads from every nearby table.

And there it was. The reason she had to eat the last two wings in front of her, despite every cell in her tongue, nose, eyes, and stomach protesting.

She grabbed another wing, holding it gingerly, despite the protection the rubber gloves afforded her from the lava disguised as sauce. She held it to her mouth, pressed her teeth together, trying to keep her searing lips from touching the spicy red buffalo sauce.

Her stomach revolted.

She dropped the wing and pressed away from the table, pulling the gloves off and making a mad dash toward the restrooms. Groans and laughter sounded from the table behind her, but she ignored them.

It was over. She'd already lost the challenge. And thankfully, the admission that she wasn't going to try to force one more bite into it had her stomach settling without any further objections.

She washed her hands and wiped away the moisture streaming from her eyes and nose. One glance in the mirror confirmed that she basically looked like a ripe cherry tomato with dark-brown hair right now, despite the cool water she'd splashed on her face.

Her mouth still stung, but she knew there was milk waiting back at the table.

However she looked right now, the promise of the soothing drink was more pressing. Plus, she wasn't a sore loser. She had to go tell Toby congratulations. And beg him not to make her pay out her bet.

A hit to her pride she could handle. She'd been a Marine, after all. Bootcamp had been a master's class in getting back up after being knocked down.

But blind dates?

Why had she been so cocky about her skills? As

though thirty years eating abuela's tamales would somehow make her immune to the spice?

She loved her abuela, but those tamales were nothing compared to this. And apparently paled in comparison to Toby's jambalaya from his home in New Orleans.

She took a deep breath and marched back out toward the table.

Applause greeted her from the table, and she curtsied with a flourish.

Tessa came around the table and handed her a glass of milk. Alexis drained the whole glass, allowing it to quench the fire inside.

"Are you okay? I've never seen that look on your face before."

Alexis nodded slowly. "Yeah, I'm all right. A little wounded pride is all."

A heavy hand clapped on her shoulder. "You did good, cher! To be honest, I only expected you to get through one!" Toby laughed heartily, and Alexis leaned in to give him a side hug.

Tessa waved to someone behind Alexis. "Hey, Jared!"

Alexis turned, her smile already spreading. The stretching skin stung a bit, her lips chapped from the hot sauce.

"What's going on here?" Jared said by way of greeting. "Looks like trouble with a capital T." He pointed at Toby with both hands, and the men laughed before shaking hands and slapping backs the way men seemed to always do.

When he finished, Jared put one arm around her. She leaned into him for a moment before he pulled away. Jared was always steady.

Adam came up next to Tessa and put his arm around her, shaking Jared's hand. "Hey, man, how's it going?"

"Good, good! I'm just picking up some takeout before I head home."

"You should join us," Tessa offered.

Alexis looked at him hopefully but saw the refusal in his face. As usual, it looked like he hadn't shaved in several days, giving him dark stubble she always wanted to feel. Would it be like sandpaper? Or softer? His short brown hair was perfectly tousled, as if he'd run his hands through it while frustrated.

"I wouldn't want to intrude. This looks like a work thing."

"We're basically done. Right, Heath?"

Alexis shut her eyes in embarrassment. The way Tessa was maneuvering the situation, she definitely had other motives.

Unfortunately, Alexis knew exactly what that motive was.

"Please, join us," Heath said with a hand wave.

"We've always got room for our friends from DK9."

Heath continued talking as Jared pulled a seat next to hers and everyone sat back down. He pointed to the wings on her plate with a questioning face. She just shook her head. She wasn't ready to tell that story quite yet.

"I was just telling an old buddy of mine about you. His daughter has an extremely severe peanut allergy. They've been living in a constant state of fear about her being exposed. I remember you trained that one dog to detect gluten, right? Think you could train one for peanuts?"

Jared slung his arm around the back of her chair, leaning back and kicking one foot up on his other knee.

"Yeah, we could definitely do that. I even saw some research recently about training dogs to detect artificial colors."

"Seriously? They can do that?" Alexis let her amazement show.

Jared flashed a smile her way, and her heart jumped into action. Probably heartburn from the wings. "I'm telling you, these animals are incredible." He turned back to Heath. "I've actually got the perfect dog in mind. You want to get me his contact info? I'd like to start as soon as possible."

Alexis watched her friend with pride as he talked with Heath, Toby, Adam and the rest of the team from Got Your Six. She knew Tessa had pushed for the invitation because she saw it as her mission to push Alexis into a relationship with Jared. But Jared was one of her best friends here in Freedom. He had been for four years, ever since she moved here.

Tessa was the other.

But there were things even Tessa and Jared didn't know about her. And as good of a friend as Jared was, that was all they would ever be.

Moving here had been a last resort. Retiring from the Marines after eight years hadn't been the plan, nor had moving in with her mother. And then–ever-so-politely–being asked to leave.

Apparently, despite her best efforts, none of Alexis's plans ever worked out.

Instead, she was left with calling in a favor from an old friend to get a job in Freedom, Colorado and a handful of prescriptions to help manage the ghosts of her past.

"Oh, Alexis!" Tessa's excited voice came from down the table. "Did I tell you? I signed us both up for the Secret Santa event that Trudy is hosting."

Alexis whirled her head around so quickly she should have whiplash. "Say again?"

"Yeah! Trudy said she's been dreaming this up for years, but things finally came together! She said there are over two hundred people signed up."

Jared shifted in his chair. "I heard something about that. What was it, four gifts or something?"

Tessa nodded. "Yeah. One each week from Thanksgiving to Christmas. I can't wait to see who I get to spoil." She nudged Adam. "I couldn't convince this guy to participate. But the rest of you, sign-up doesn't close until Sunday night."

"I can't believe she signed me up," Alexis whispered to Jared.

He chuckled. "Oh, come on. Yes, you can. It's Tessa."

He was right. It was Tessa, and she had a good heart, though sometimes misguided. In this case, she probably thought Alexis needed to make new friends or participate in the community or some of the other things she was always spouting.

"Are you doing it?" she asked hopefully. If Jared was participating, maybe she could just buy him presents. It'd be way less awkward than a random stranger in town she hadn't met. Freedom was a small town, but she'd managed to fly pretty well under the radar for four years. And she was perfectly fine with that.

Jared shook his head. "Wasn't planning on it. Sounds pretty hokey. And doesn't this town already have enough Christmas events? Between the gingerbread house competition and all the parties?" He started numbering them off on his fingers. "Carol-

8

ing. Bake sale. Parade. The dance fundraiser. Should I keep going?" He raised an eyebrow.

Alexis groaned. "Ugh. Fine. You at least have to help me buy gifts for my match."

Jared smiled, his dark eyes glinting with amusement. "Whatever you need, Alex."

She softened. Everyone else in Freedom seemed intent on ignoring her instructions to call her Alex. Alexis it was. But sometimes, Jared called her Alex, and it felt like a secret between them. "Thanks. I knew I could count on you."

"Always," he confirmed with a soft tone only she could hear.

Her stomach flipped, like it usually did when Jared said anything remotely intimate.

How he was still single was beyond her. She'd heard the tale of Melody, who left him just before Christmas a few years back. She'd often wondered if he was still hung up on her, but she'd never asked.

And even though Tessa was convinced they belonged together, Alexis knew that Jared, with his happy-go-lucky demeanor and playful spirit, deserved someone just as whole.

She, on the other hand, was hopelessly damaged.

Sure, the medications were working. For the most part, she could manage without the major episodes of anxiety or depression that had marked her life after the service. But they were still there. It was still a part of her.

And she wasn't going to drag anyone down with her.

Especially not Jared.

"I've got your first date lined up," Toby leaned around Jared to tell her.

She saw Jared's eyebrows shoot skyward and felt herself blush.

"It's a long story," she said

"I think I've got time for this one," he responded with a laugh lacing his words.

Alexis buried her head in her hands and leaned forward on her knees.

"Toby gets to set me up on ten blind dates." Her answer was muffled by her hands.

Jared must have gotten the idea though, because his exclamation of surprise made her groan. Toby eagerly filled in the details, regaling Jared with the events of the evening.

He placed a hand on her back, scratching it gently. It felt wonderful, but she could feel him shaking with laughter next to her, which almost ruined the sweet gesture.

Almost.

She couldn't blame him for laughing. It was ridiculous. She was ridiculous. And now she had ten dates in six weeks.

Plus a Secret Santa who would be leaving her annoying presents. Probably fruity-scented lotions that would give her a headache or cheap holiday trinkets. Yay.

Merry Christmas to her.

2
_____

*G*rowing up in Colorado meant that Jared was born wearing a Denver Broncos jersey. When a connection from the Denver Police Department offered him a set of tickets to Sunday's game, Jared jumped at the chance. And then he called Alexis.

With her navy-blue-and-orange stocking cap pulled around her head and long strands of dark hair trailing around her shoulders, Jared could barely take his eyes off Alexis to watch the game.

He couldn't stop thinking about Toby and these stupid blind dates. What was he going to do? He'd considered calling Toby and trying to talk him out of it. But the odds of the stubborn Cajun giving in were slim to none.

"Come on! That was pass interference!" Alexis

yelled toward the field, along with most of the stadium, judging by the sudden outburst of boos. She turned to him. "Did you see that?"

Jared nodded, though he hadn't seen much of anything. The third quarter ended and the crowd uproar dissipated as it became clear that the refs weren't changing their mind on the call. Jared watched absently as the big screen played a highlight reel of tackles from the game.

"You want some of my nachos?" he offered as the highlights ended and the music switched.

Alexis grabbed one from the tray and grinned. "Thanks. And thanks for the ticket. I haven't been to a game in ages. I forget how fun they are. All the energy."

"I'm glad it worked out. This time of year is so crazy for everybody."

Alexis was telling him what Toby had planned for her first few blind dates, when the people around them started yelling.

"It's you guys! Kiss her!"

Jared looked around in confusion, then recognized himself and Alexis being shown on the Jumbotron.

"Kiss!"

He looked to his right and saw Alexis's face, wide-eyed and completely frozen, apparently having seen the same thing he did. "Uhh, what should we do?" he asked, but she didn't respond.

He had no idea she was so stage shy. He nudged her knee. "Hey. Look at me," he said.

Finally, she turned to him. There was clapping and whistling and yells happening all around them, but Jared just met her eyes and saw a vulnerability in Alexis he hadn't seen before.

"Hey, it's okay. Just look at me, okay?" He glanced back up at the giant screen, hoping they'd moved on to another couple, but their faces were still there.

He tried to wave the camera away, but people just cheered louder. Oh come on. Couldn't they see it wasn't going to happen?

"Come on! Kiss her, man!"

Jared's mind raced, looking for a solution. Should he kiss her on the cheek? Start licking his nacho cheese ferociously to draw the attention away from her?

Alexis's eyes were on his. She was trusting him to get her out of this.

He pulled her hand into his and kissed it. Then he looked to see if the camera had moved on, but it was still zeroed in on them.

The playful strains of "Kiss the Girl" from *Little Mermaid* mocked him. He'd love to be in the place where he could casually lean over and plant a kiss on her lips, like the other dozen couples who'd probably been on the screen before.

Frustrated at his own inaction when it came to his feelings about Alexis and about the cameraman who couldn't seem to take a hint, Jared decided what he needed to do.

He looked toward the camera, held up a finger as if to say 'wait one second,' and gave a big wink, drawing laughter from the crowd. He pulled off his baseball hat, holding it in front of their faces as he leaned in close to her. As far as anyone else could tell, he was happily kissing her behind the hat.

Within the privacy of the shadow of his hat, he studied her eyes. "You okay?"

She nodded, but didn't say anything. He hoped she was okay with this.

There were cheers from the crowd at his action. Jared held up his other arm and pumped his fist up and down as if there had been some victory.

"Just smile when I pull the hat away, okay?"

It seemed like Alexis had snapped out of the shock she was in. "I can do that," she confirmed.

When he pulled the hat down, Alexis smiled and waved to the crowd. Jared gave a thumbs-up and watched in relief as the camera panned to another victim.

"Man, they are relentless, aren't they?"

Alexis grabbed another nacho from the tray in his lap. "Next time, it'd probably be easier to just lean over and kiss me."

Jared whipped his head back toward her. "Say again?" He used the military phrase she often pulled out when she wanted him to repeat something.

Next to him, Alexis was acting completely casual. He must have misheard something. She pointed to the screen where the kiss cam was still finding unsuspecting couples to harass. "Look at this. These people barely even kiss. Two seconds and the camera leaves." She shrugged. "If you just lean in and give a peck, they're on their way."

Jared searched for words. "Are you saying you wish I would have kissed you?"

Alexis rolled her eyes at him. "Not like that! I'm just saying… It would have been easier."

Jared frowned. "Well yeah, it would have been easier! But you weren't talking to me, and I couldn't just kiss you without permission. So I improvised."

Alexis leaned toward him, nudging his shoulder. "You're totally right. I'm sorry. I don't like being the center of attention."

"I know," he said quietly.

"You're a good friend, Jared Keen."

He stuffed a nacho in his mouth to keep himself from saying anything more. Like that he was done pretending that he didn't have feelings for Alexis. Or that the idea of her going on a blind date with anyone had been driving him crazy for days.

J<small>ARED LOOKED</small> left and right down the sidewalk before ducking inside Watkins Real Estate, Trudy's office on the square in the center of town. Desperate times called for desperate measures, right?

A chime on the door jingled as it shut behind him and a voice called from out of sight. "I'll be right there!" Jared looked around the cheerfully decorated office. One half was still decked out in autumn decor, with pumpkins and leaves in the center of a large conference table. The other half had already been usurped by Christmas. A small tree in silver and blue sat in the corner, and lighted garland trimmed the desks.

He turned when a voice greeted him. "Hello, how can I help you?"

Jared held out his hand to the well-dressed woman. "Hi, are you Trudy?"

She nodded with a bright smile. "At your service."

His nerves rose and Jared took a deep breath, scuffing his boot on the floor. He flashed a confident smile to hide his nerves. "I'm Jared. I guess I haven't met before."

"I don't believe we have. Nice to meet you, Jared."

"The pleasure is all mine. I'm actually here about the Secret Santa event. Rumor has it that you are the woman to talk to." He winked at her. Jared had always known how to turn on the charm. It made him a favorite of the secretaries at school.

Trudy's cheeks reddened, and her eyes brightened even further. She clasped her hands together. "Oh, that's wonderful. Let me get my notebook and we'll get you signed up." She moved toward the desk and pulled a binder from the surface.

Jared gritted his teeth. This was harder than he thought. "Actually, Trudy, I had a question." He cleared his throat. "About how the pairs are made?"

Trudy paused. "Oh?"

Jared rubbed the back of his head with his hand, then lowered his arm. He gave a sheepish smile. "You see, there's a woman."

"Ah," came Trudy's soft exhale of understanding.

"She's my best friend, but it's more than that. And I'm hoping you might help me show her how I feel by arranging for me to be her Secret Santa?" Jared rushed through the request, feeling more ridiculous by the minute. Hearing Toby talking about setting Alexis up on not one but ten dates this Christmas had him nearly green with envy. He hated the idea of her dating anyone. This Secret Santa idea was probably like throwing a fourth quarter Hail Mary pass. Too little, too late. But he refused to believe he'd missed his chance.

It felt like an eternity before Trudy reacted. He nearly bolted toward the door.

Trudy put a hand to her heart, the binder underneath it. "Oh, that's the most romantic thing I've ever heard."

He released a huge sigh of relief. "So you'll help me?"

Her eyes softened. "Oh, Jared. I wish I could. Truly! But I can't let people choose who they are paired with. It would ruin the integrity of the whole event."

Disappointment washed over him, but he forced a smile. "Oh. That's okay. I understand."

"Can I still sign you up for the event?" She looked hopeful. "The more the merrier, right?"

He held up his hands in front of him. "Oh, I don't know. Probably not."

Trudy patted his arm. "You never know. Maybe the Lord will be on your side when it comes to the pairings."

Jared considered her words. She had a point. Maybe he shouldn't try to force it. Heaven knew that had gotten him enough heartache in the past. If it was meant to be, maybe God would help him with the opportunity. And he would do everything he could not to mess it up by coming on too strong.

What was the worst that could happen? He picked out some meaningless gifts for someone who wasn't Alexis. Maybe he could even rope her into shopping with him.

"Yeah, okay. Why not? Sign me up."

"Excellent! I'll just get some information from you and we'll be all set."

He filled out the registration form, racking his brain for things to write in the categories, like hobbies and a list of favorite colors, foods, and desserts. At least they gave any gift giver something to go on. He wrote "Pumpkin Snickerdoodles from Stories and Scones" on the dessert line in his typical messy scrawl. His Secret Santa could leave him four boxes of those as the four gifts and he'd be thrilled.

He wondered what Alexis's sheet looked like. Of course, Tessa had probably filled it out. Would it be accurate?

"Okay, Jared. You're all set. You'll receive an email with your Secret Santa assignment. Remember, your goal is to bless the person you are giving to, and try to guess who is leaving gifts for you!"

"All right. Thanks, Trudy. Oh, and thanks for putting this all together. It must be a ton of work."

She laughed heartily. "Oh, yes. It is. But it is giving this old woman something to stay busy with this season. Some might say Freedom doesn't need any more Christmas festivities, but I've always loved a good Secret Santa exchange." Her face grew serious. "Besides, for some people, these might be the only gifts they receive this year."

Something in her voice made Jared wonder if perhaps that was the case for Trudy herself.

"Well, I'm sure it's going to be wonderful."

She smiled again. "Even if you don't get your young lady as your assignment, I'm sure you'll find another way to tell her how you feel."

"I'll definitely be praying about that, Trudy. We'll just have to see."

"Good luck!" she called after him as he exited the office.

Jared climbed back in his truck and headed toward DK9.

That hadn't gone how he'd hoped, but it wasn't all bad. He was going to keep his hopes low. He probably wasn't going to be Alexis's Secret Santa. But he was determined to have fun either way. He could see how much the event meant to Trudy.

Secret Santa was the perfect event for a town like Freedom. This close-knit community never did anything halfway. There were sure to be some extravagant–and likely some hilarious–gifts exchanged during the month-long event.

Pulling into the parking lot at DK9, Jared tried to push thoughts of Alexis from his mind. He should probably just accept that they would always just be friends. The last thing he wanted to do was push. That's what had driven Melody away. From the painful phone call they'd had six months later, he'd learned that she thought he was too intense, clingy, and moving too fast.

That was super fun to mull over while he still had the engagement ring he'd bought for her.

If he was going to tell Alexis how he felt, he was going to make sure not to make the same mistakes he'd made with Melody. Especially because Alexis was likely to be even more resistant to the idea.

When she'd moved to town, they'd connected over a shared love of the Dodgers one morning at church. She invited him to a game in Denver when they'd come to town to play the Rockies. And a friendship was born.

But never anything more. She made it very clear that she wasn't interested. Sometimes, he still wondered though. When she let down her guard, he would swear there was interest there. Or was it all wishful thinking? Maybe his imagination was just running wild, looking for feelings that weren't there. Just like he'd thought Melody was as in love as he was when he bought the ring and planned the romantic Christmas Eve proposal he never got to give.

He waved to Amber, the assistant trainer who'd been at DK9 for nearly a decade. She was great with the dogs and was working on her professional certification right now. He watched over the half-wall that separated the training room from the hallway to the offices as she worked with one of the younger dogs, Harley, on simple obedience commands. Amber rewarded Harley with treats from a pouch on her waist each time the dog obeyed.

Jared stopped at Derek's office door when he saw his boss was already in. "Hey, man. How's it going?"

Derek Held looked up from his computer. "Not bad, man. Trying to book flights to Alabama for Thanksgiving. Crazy expensive."

Jared smiled. "Yeah, but you'll still buy them. Megan missing her family?"

Derek's wife, Megan, was an author. She'd come to Freedom six years ago on a writing trip and ended up staying. Her family was still in Alabama though.

"Yeah. She's also complaining about it being too cold, of course." Derek rolled his eyes, but Jared saw the love in the good-natured complaint.

"Aw, man. It's just getting good. I was thinking about taking Phoenix out on a hike tomorrow morning. Maybe hide something in one of Pete's cabins if he'll let us."

"I'll give him a call and see if he's got one available. Maybe you can do Hollywood's final exam while you're there?"

Jared nodded. "I could do that. Is Atlanta ready for him?"

"They're calling weekly looking for updates."

"Oh, that reminds me. Heath was telling me

about a friend who might be interested in a peanut-detection dog. I was thinking Ruby might be a good candidate. Her nose is one of the best I've ever seen, and the handler would be a teenage girl. I think they'd have good chemistry."

Derek nodded. "I think she's a great fit. Bring them in and start the process. I'll let you take the lead."

Jared filled with satisfaction at the confidence Derek had in him. After seven years, they were partners more than they were employee and boss. Someday soon, Jared hoped to make the partnership official. "Sounds good."

As he settled into his office, his phone chimed with a text message.

Alexis: My first date is tonight.

Jared frowned at the reminder. In the four years he'd known Alexis, she'd never been on a date. He'd definitely been paying attention. Still, he couldn't exactly let her know how much it was messing with him that she was going to go on a date with not one, but ten different guys. He crafted the perfect snarky reply.

Jared: Surely you've been on a date before.

Alexis: Very funny. I mean my first blind date from Toby's stupid bet. Apparently, I have a date with someone named Cory. He's Pastor Stephens' nephew?

Jared chuckled at the message. Everybody knew

24

and loved Pastor Stephens. But his nephew was an odd duck, to say the least.

Jared: Have fun with that.

Jared: Text me from the bathroom if you need rescuing.

Alexis: Hopefully it won't come to that.

Jared smiled and sent an animated picture with a young girl giving a thumbs-up. The caption read "You've got this."

In his experience, Alexis could handle just about anything. Cory Stephens, though? What was Toby thinking?

3

*A*lexis grabbed another chip from the bowl on the table, taking a tiny bite from the corner as she listened to Cory drone on about the current state of the slopes at Freedom Ridge Resort. They'd been sitting for less than five minutes and his froggy voice was already driving her crazy. He'd swiped at his nose with a napkin no less than four times.

"...just not the same as last year. We need a really good snow event. I'm–" Cory interrupted his sermon to blow his nose into his napkin. The blaring foghorn of mucus made Alexis turn beet red in embarrassment. Half a dozen heads turned toward their table, and she slid farther down into the booth.

"If you're not feeling well, maybe we should just call it a night," she offered. She really did feel a little bad for Cory. Besides, Toby never said how long the dates had to be. Five minutes definitely counted. If she'd been smarter, she would have convinced Toby to count the football game with Jared as one of her dates. With the whole kiss cam debacle, it should have definitely counted.

She'd been so embarrassed at how she'd reacted, but Jared was as cool as a cucumber, of course. Part of her wished he would have just kissed her, but she knew his honor wouldn't have let him do that. Still, being there tucked behind his hat when fifty thousand people assumed they were kissing had been surprisingly intimate.

Just the sort of feeling she probably needed to avoid with Jared. She refocused on her date, hoping he'd agree to go home early.

"Oh, no. I'm fine," he insisted with a stuffy tone. "It's just...allerg–ACHOO!" He sneezed forcefully, even as he was reaching for the napkin again. Too late. Alexis gingerly set her chip back on the table and pushed the basket of chips, now covered in his sniffly, sneezy germs, toward him.

"Tell me about yourself, Lexi."

"It's Alexis," she corrected, emphasizing the first syllable.

"Potato, potahto," he said, blowing his nose again.

She grimaced. She would do her best to overlook his cold, because that wasn't his fault. But disrespectful and boring weren't things that would fade when the germs were gone.

"I joined the Marines right out of high school. Now I work at Got Your Six with Toby and the gang."

Cory opened his mouth and then shut it again. She watched blankly, raising her eyebrows as the pause grew longer. Finally, he squeaked out, "Ma- Marine?" Then he seemed to recover. "I knew you worked at Got Your Six. I just assumed you were the office manager or something. Personally, I think women in the military is an abomination, you know?"

Alexis floundered for a moment, unsure she'd heard him correctly.

"I don't know what they were thinking, allowing women to serve," he continued. His momentary surprise had apparently faded and Cory was on a roll. One that made her want to roll him down the mountain.

The server walked up and stood next to the table, notepad in hand. "Have you decided what you're having?"

Alexis glanced up with a tight smile, grateful for the interruption. "Actually, I'll be going now." She looked back at her date. "It was nice to meet you, Cory, but it's clear this isn't going to work. I recom- mend Claritin for the allergies. Unfortunately, I don't think there is a cure for the misogyny. Have a great night!"

With that as her farewell, Alexis hurried out of El Cresta. Which was disappointing because she'd really been looking forward to some enchiladas. She headed toward the fast-food Mexican joint that would surely be a poor substitute for El Cresta. It would have to do. Her route took her past DK9, and she spotted Jared's truck still in the lot.

She hit the button to voice-dial him. When he answered, she said, "I'm getting Taco Bravo. Are you hungry?"

Jared's surprise was evident in his voice. "What happened to your date with Cory? Did he stand you up?"

"If only. It was a total bust, but at least it counts. One down, nine to go. So, do you want tacos or what? I saw your truck at work."

Jared sighed. "Yeah, I should eat. You know what I like."

Alexis recited the order from memory. "Two chalupa grandes with no sour cream and a Diet Coke." They'd eaten takeout from this particular restaurant enough times for her to know that Jared always ordered the same thing. A creature of habit.

She, on the other hand, liked to mix it up. She changed her coffee creamer with the seasons, never listened to the same playlist for more than a week, and was a sucker for the limited-time special at a restaurant.

"I'll see you in a few minutes," she said, disconnecting the call as she pulled into the drive-thru.

When she parked next to Jared's truck less than ten minutes later, the smell of spicy meat and nacho cheese filled the car, encouraged by the warm air blowing from the vents. Jared came to her door and opened it. She handed him the bag of food and grabbed their drinks. "Thanks," she said.

"Come on in and tell me all about your date. I'm dying of curiosity."

She rolled her eyes and groaned as she followed him in the door of DK9 Training. "I'd rather just forget it ever happened."

"And you can. Just as soon as you tell me everything." Jared looked back and winked.

"How does that work? I'm the one who brought you food, and you're still trying to boss me around."

"Ahh, yes. But you're the one who called me. Which means you actually *want* to talk about it, despite your insistence to the contrary."

She narrowed her eyes and frowned at him. She considered denying it, claiming that he was wrong. But she relented. "Fine. But don't get all jealous or feel like you have to defend my honor."

Jared froze. "Did something happen that I would

need to defend your honor?" There was ice in his voice as he asked the question.

Alexis felt a tug of appreciation for his protective instincts, however unnecessary it might be. "Settle down, tiger. I'm fine. Just some pigheaded comments. That's why the date ended so early."

Maverick, a lovable golden lab she'd met before, greeted her with a wagging tail, gently knocking against the leg of the chair.

"Hey, Mav. Who's a good boy?" The tail thumping intensified, and she reached down to pat his head. "How's this guy doing?"

Jared tipped his head to the side. "He's an amazing dog. Very intuitive. But I don't think his nose is cut out for any of our jobs. I don't know for sure yet. He hasn't failed yet, but I'm pretty good by now at telling who is going to cut it. Maybe he'd be a good support dog for someone. I'll have to think about it."

Alexis slid him his drink, and he pulled their food from the brown paper bag.

Jared started unwrapping his meal. "Okay, okay. Start at the beginning, and I'll try to decide if Cory needs a little reminder to behave himself after the fact."

≈

Jared tucked into his chalupas, while Alexis recounted her story. He cringed at the sneeze and the nose-blowing.

She became even more animated as she told the rest. "When he finally got around to talking about something other than the snow conditions on the mountain, I told him that I was a Marine and it totally threw him for a loop. He basically glitched for a minute and then spouted off all this nonsense about how women didn't belong in the military."

Yikes. No wonder Alexis was fired up. "Oh, please." Jared could see why she had ended the date early. "I'm sorry he feels that way, and I'm sorry he said that to you. How dense do you have to be?"

Alexis sipped her soda. "I know! It was like he thought I was going to agree with him. Even after everything I experienced, the good and the bad, I don't regret my decision. And I still look up to so many incredible women who served or are serving. It was just... that was the last straw. I just left." She held up her taco. "Hence the backup dinner plan."

He chuckled. "Yeah, it's not El Cresta, but it'll do in a pinch." Then he flashed a flirtatious smile. "Besides, the excellent company makes up for the lackluster cuisine."

Alexis blushed and laughed softly. He was filled with pleasure at being able to make her laugh so easily, especially after such a rough evening. She didn't disagree with his assertion, either.

Time with Alexis was just so effortless. No pretense, no judgment. Exactly how he thought it should be. It was far from what he remembered with Melody. He was always on his best behavior, hoping for a scrap of attention from her, always doing things that she wanted to keep her happy.

"So, what has you working so late tonight?"

Jared looked through the window to the unoccupied training area. "I'm making a training plan for a new client. It's that one Heath mentioned. Kyle and his daughter are coming into town next week to meet Ruby and see if she's a good fit."

"That's so cool. I hope you can help her. That sounds super scary."

He nodded. It was a blessing that Kyle was able to afford the cost of the service dog. Training was an expensive process with lots of man hours. And the cost had to cover some of the time training dogs who never made it through the program. Unfortunately, they couldn't do it for free.

Jared had always felt a lot of guilt when providing estimates to potential owners. It was one thing to charge the government twenty thousand dollars. It was another to tell Laura that a seizure detection dog for her seven-year-old was going to require them to take out a second mortgage.

He looked back over the training facility and brought up the idea that had been on his heart for a year or two. "What would you think about a non-profit branch of DK9? One that people could donate to and help cover some of the cost of service dogs for those who can't afford them?"

"I think that's an amazing idea," she said. Her voice rang with a pure tone and a hint of admiration.

He turned from the window to look at her expression. She was looking at him with wide eyes and a pleased expression of surprise. "You think so?"

She nodded emphatically. "Absolutely. What an amazing opportunity to help more people. Plus, I think there are tons of people in and around Freedom that would love to get more involved in what you guys do here. Most people know about the search and rescue dogs, since you always get news coverage for lost hikers and such, but I think the other things you do are equally impressive. A non-profit operation would give everyone a chance to support you."

Jared hadn't considered that side of things. He was just hoping it would give him a chance to tell Laura and her seven-year-old that they could apply for the cost of the dog to be at least partially funded.

"Thanks. I might spend some more time thinking about how this could work and then talk to Derek about it."

Maybe Jared wasn't really meant to be a partner with Derek in DK9. Perhaps he was supposed to take DK9 in a different direction and take on leadership within that.

"I'll be praying about it for you," Alexis offered.

He smiled at her kindness. "I really appreciate that. Thanks."

"Of course."

"How are you doing? Are you headed home for the holidays?" Thanksgiving was next week, and then Christmas would be right around the corner.

Alexis shook her head, covering her mouth with her hand to show she was chewing. "Nah. You know Mom and I aren't on good terms. It's easier just to send a card."

Jared frowned. "I'm sorry. That's got to be tough. You know you're always welcome with me and my parents."

She shrugged. "We'll see. Jan and Pete usually invite me to her house, too. But your parents are cool."

His eyebrows flicked upward. He wouldn't exactly call his parents 'cool.' But he loved them. Since Dad had retired last year, they'd been traveling all over the United States, visiting half a dozen National Parks so far.

"Well, they get back from Northern California

this weekend. Mom's already got her pies ordered from Jan, I think."

Alexis didn't answer, so Jared prodded again. "What do you say? You, me, my parents, and my renegade younger brother?"

She chuckled at his description. "The cowboy, right?"

He nodded. "Yep." Jason was still playing cowboy at some ranch over in western Colorado–when he wasn't throwing his hat in the ring at rodeos all over the southwest.

She sipped her soda, and his eyes flipped to the movement of her lips. He forced himself to pull them back up to her eyes. "Sure. Thanksgiving dinner sounds good."

Jared smiled, but he didn't let more of the crazy celebration happening inside show on his face. He wanted to fist pump and jump up and down. Instead, he took another bite after replying with a simple, "Cool."

He knew it was a big step. Alexis had met his parents, but Thanksgiving dinner was different, wasn't it? But he wasn't going to scare her away by making a big deal out of it. Maybe he was the only one who thought anything of it. Friends joined friends for holiday dinners all the time.

But not Alexis. And he'd certainly never invited anyone. The last guest at their holiday dinner had been Melody. They all knew how that had turned out.

"So one date down, eh?"

Alexis nodded. "Yeah. Apparently, I have one next week and one at the Christmas tree lighting ceremony."

Jared pressed his lips together in disappointment. The tree lighting was a pretty romantic date. The Christmas lights and the music and huddling close to keep warm after dark. He definitely didn't like that Alexis would be there with someone else.

"Any idea who they are yet?" He kept his tone casual, pretending that he wouldn't be running background checks on each date the moment she left tonight.

But Alexis shook her head. "Not yet. Honestly, I don't feel like it matters. This whole thing is like a bad movie."

"How do you mean?"

"It's a waste of time. I'm not going to find love on a blind date that Toby sets up. I could date every man in Freedom and I still wouldn't end up married with two-point-five kids like Tessa thinks I need."

"So what? You never want to find someone to be with forever?" Jared couldn't hide his dismay at this revelation. He'd spent the better part of the last eight years trying to find the one God had for him.

Alexis shook her head. "I just don't think it's that big of a deal, you know? I'm fine on my own."

This woman was stubborn. He'd known that for a long time. But maybe he had underestimated how much so.

"Well, yeah. But just because you're fine doesn't mean it couldn't be better."

Alexis just frowned at him. "I disagree."

He had to tone it down. She obviously wasn't interested in him, because if she was, she wouldn't be so adamant about never settling down. She wasn't even leaving the door open the tiniest crack for a relationship with anyone. So maybe it was time he just admitted it wasn't going to happen and move on.

Maybe he needed someone to set him up on ten blind dates.

Right now, a random stranger being the one for him seemed just as likely as Alexis learning of his feelings in a way that didn't scare her off. Not to mention the absolute long shot of her reciprocating them.

He needed a Christmas miracle.

4

_____

*a*lexis pulled her enchiladas from the oven, wrapped the casserole dish in a large towel, and loaded it into the car. Abuela would never forgive her if she showed up to someone's house empty-handed. She was inexplicably nervous about today's festivities.

Not that she should be. Jared was sweet to invite her. And she'd met his parents, since they attended Freedom Bible Church as well. But going to their house felt different.

She shook her head to clear her negative thoughts as she shifted into reverse. Had she taken her medication this morning? She tried to remember but couldn't. With a sigh, she put the car back in park and jogged inside.

She pulled the prescription bottle from the medicine cabinet, then paused as she started to open the lid. "No, I already took it," she said out loud.

But what if she was misremembering? The last thing she wanted was to have a panic attack in the middle of Thanksgiving dinner with Jared's family. On normal days, her routine was very predictable, but holidays always threw her off.

"Come on, Alexis," she said to her reflection. "Think about this morning. What did you do?"

She mentally walked through her steps since waking up. Thirty seconds later, she threw her hands up. She'd definitely taken the medicine. She remembered throwing away her old toothbrush and getting a new one just before taking it. The old toothbrush sat on the top of the trash as a confirmation.

She jogged back down to the garage to her waiting car.

At Jared's house, she paused in front of the door. Maybe she should just turn around and go home. She could eat the entire tray of enchiladas and call it a day. Watch the Saints play football so she could trash talk with Toby about it next week.

She turned back toward the car.

The front door opened as she turned and she jumped, whirling back around and trying to look like she hadn't just been about to bail.

"Hey!" Jared's exuberant greeting washed away

all her anxious thoughts about the day. How could she have wanted to leave instead of hanging out with him? "I thought I heard a car door out here. Come on, get inside before you freeze."

She followed him inside, admiring the way his black sweater emphasized the build of his arms and shoulders. He took the casserole dish from her hands and the soft sweater grazed her fingertips. Was that cashmere?

"Well, if it isn't GI Jane."

Alexis turned toward the living room and saw Jared's younger brother. At least, she could assume that's who it was. The similarity was striking, though Jason had none of Jared's kind features and playfulness. He was all hard lines and angles. He reclined in the armchair, his cowboy hat on his lap and his hands clasped behind his head.

"Shut up, Jason," came Jared's warning reply as he returned without the casserole. Was that animosity in his tone?

"It's fine. I can handle it," she reassured him. "You must be the rodeo champion I've heard so much about."

"Ha." The scornful laugh cut through the room. "Something like that, I suppose." Jason pulled his hat and covered his face with it, leaning the chair even farther back.

Jared rolled his eyes. "Just ignore him. He wasn't raised in a barn, but I think he lives in one now."

Jason held up an obscene hand gesture that made Alexis cringe. Luckily, Jared didn't see it. He grabbed her hand. "Come on. Mom and Dad are in the kitchen."

It was kind of reassuring to know that her family wasn't the only one that was kind of messed up. There were a lot of happy families here. Sometimes, it made her feel like a bad Christian that her own relationships weren't that healthy.

But she knew Jared and his parents loved the Lord deeply. And that they loved Jason, despite the challenge of it. Jared really seemed to struggle with how to handle his brother's behavior.

She loved her family too. But her mom had really hurt her. It was as if her mom thought PTSD wasn't real. Or if it was real, then Alexis had brought it on herself by signing up for the Marines in the first place. Which meant her mother wasn't going to tolerate any of the hard parts of living with it.

So Alexis had called Heath, found a job, and gotten some really good help from doctors in Denver. Her PTSD was better managed right now, but she wasn't sure she'd ever be able to forgive her mom for not being there when she needed her.

Or trust that anyone else would truly be able to

handle the dark parts of the disorder if and when it flared up again.

For today though, her medicine was working, despite the low-level anxiety that came from being with unfamiliar people in an unfamiliar place. It was a normal response and manageable.

She took a deep breath before following Jared into the kitchen.

"Happy Thanksgiving. I'm so glad you decided to join us." Jared's mom had medium-length dark hair with a streak of silver at the front that almost looked intentional, it was so stylish.

Alexis glanced at Jared. "He didn't really let me say no. But I appreciate the invitation. Your home is lovely."

Jared's smile faltered. "You didn't have to come," he said, his voice laced with something like frustration.

She laid her hand on his shoulder. "I didn't mean it like that. I just meant..." She tried to explain. "It's good that you are persistent. Because I'm stubborn. You know that," she said playfully, nudging his hip with her own.

His smile returned, filling her with relief. She hadn't meant to upset him. In fact, she hated that she'd been the cause of his carefree joy to fade, even for a moment.

That was why they could never work. He was all

sunshine and happiness. And she was dark clouds and lightning bolts–even with her medication. She'd never been a rainbows and positivity kind of gal.

It certainly helped in her career, where a certain amount of pessimism helped you prepare for the worst. But it wasn't exactly fun to be around.

Sure, she could fake it to an extent. And it was probably one reason she gravitated to people like Jared and Tessa, trying to absorb some of their inner light by osmosis. And it sometimes worked–while she was with them.

But then she had to go home.

JARED TRIED NOT to dwell on Alexis's comment about him forcing her to come to Thanksgiving. Had he? Apparently, he would never learn his lesson. First Melody, now Alexis, and he was doing the same thing–coming on too strong and not letting them breathe.

But she had come. And even though Jason was a jerk, she seemed to have a good time. She laughed at his dad's jokes, despite the fact that they weren't remotely funny. She seemed genuinely entertained.

Around mid-afternoon, he walked her back out to her car, holding her now-empty casserole dish. He was so tempted to say something. Just a hint to plant the seed that he was interested and saw her as so much more than a friend.

"I'm really glad you came today. I hope you had a good time."

"I did. Thanks again for inviting me." She wrapped her arms around him and gave him a hug. He squeezed tightly for a moment, not wanting to let go. But he did, because Alexis was as unaffected as ever, giving a perfectly friendly hug with no sign of wanting to linger.

"Alexis?" He said her name as she opened the car door, and she turned back, already halfway inside.

"Yeah?"

Her dark eyes met his, and the copper flecks glinted in the afternoon light. There was so much he wanted to say. Declarations that had been building for four years on the tip of his tongue. He wanted to tell her to stay. To curl up together and watch a movie on the couch. Spend the day and come back tomorrow. Things were better when they were together.

But he couldn't say all that.

So he swallowed heavily. "Drive safely."

She smiled and climbed inside. "See you later."

He watched her drive away, his fists pressed into his pockets. If this wasn't going to happen, then he needed God to take away these feelings. It was too hard.

Friday morning, he held his phone overhead as he lay on his back, still in bed and entirely unmotivated to change the fact. He was greeted with an unfamiliar email address in his inbox. "Your Anonymous Angel Assignment."

Clicking into the email, he scanned the information. His breath caught in his throat. In his surprise, his fingers lost their grip and he dropped the phone, wincing when it fell directly on his face.

"Oh, ow." He grabbed the phone and rolled to his stomach to reread the information. Surely, he'd been imagining it.

But as he scrolled again, he saw the same assignment.

Alexis Alonzo

32 years old

Interests: flowers, gardening, coffee, yarn and crafts

JARED RAISED his eyebrows at the list. Tessa really had fun with this. Because he knew for a fact that Alexis thought bouquets were a waste of money and slightly depressing because their death was inevitable. She didn't garden. In fact, he didn't even think she had a houseplant. Didn't she kill every single cactus Tessa had given her?

The coffee part was true. And the yarn? Well, he'd be shocked if it wasn't another hobby Tessa thought Alexis should cultivate instead of one she really had.

If Jared had filled out the questionnaire, it would have read more like "hiking, eating, arguing, reading, and weapons."

Not that putting weapons on your Secret Santa exchange would be a great look.

He read the email again for the third time, a huge grin on his face.

He'd let go of this as a pipe dream since talking to Trudy a week and a half ago. Had she secretly intervened, despite her moral objections? Or had God really stepped in and divinely set this appointment?

Either way, Jared was going to use it. This was his chance to show Alexis how he felt about her. Without her knowing that it was him. If she seemed interested, he could reveal himself. And if she didn't? Well, maybe he'd move to Seattle.

With new energy for the day ahead, Jared leapt out of bed and got dressed. He had some planning and shopping to do.

5

---

*A*lexis clutched her hot chocolate with both hands. It was a strategic move. Not only would it keep her fingertips from freezing, but it would keep her date, Brad, from trying to grab her hand again.

Apparently, the guy couldn't take a hint.

He was nice enough, but she didn't want to hold anyone's hand. Her conscience niggled in disagreement with the thought. The truth was she would love to hold Jared's hand again. He grabbed it once while he was leading her to the kitchen at his parents' house on Thanksgiving. It wasn't the first time he had casually grabbed her hand, either. It always left her feeling a bit jittery and unsettled. And wanting to rejoin their clasp whenever he let go.

Brad though? Yeah, she didn't want to hold his slimy hand.

Coming to the Christmas tree lighting ceremony on a blind date had been a bad idea. There were hundreds of people here, and between the two of them, it seemed like they had seen every single person they knew. The number of meaningful looks she had gotten from people who were passing was way too high.

She wanted to paint a sign on her forehead that proclaimed the fact that they weren't together. At least, not in the way everyone was assuming.

Despite the less-than-ideal company for the evening, Alexis did enjoy the Christmas tree lighting event each year. It was one of those enduring traditions that the small town of Freedom somehow managed to hold onto, despite the influx of newcomers.

They found a place on a park bench and sat in awkward silence as the merry sounds of Christmas carols drifted through the air courtesy of the local high school choir. Beside her, Brad stifled a large yawn.

"Oh, I'm sorry."

Alexis smiled lightly in sympathy. "Early morning today?"

"Nah, I just stayed up until about 4 playing video games. Didn't roll out of bed until after noon, but

I'm still dragging. I don't understand why. That's a solid eight hours, you know?"

Alexis tried to hide her disbelief. Sure, sometimes she saw 4 a.m. on the clock. Occasionally, there would be a work assignment that required overnight surveillance or travel that began in the wee hours of the morning while it was still dark. But other than that, Alexis couldn't imagine there was anything she would rather be doing at four in the morning beyond sleeping. Especially if it was going to ruin the rest of her day.

"Oh," she said, "that's... fun. What game were you playing?"

Brad was yawning again. "You probably wouldn't know it. I've been playing since I was a teenager. It's an online multiplayer universe. I'm a level 300 wizard now, and I have the highest number of castle takeovers in our league. I've already finished collecting all seven of the elite dragon eggs and only need two phoenix feathers before I can craft a legendary staff, which will give me two hundred extra hit points on lightning spells."

Alexis had no idea what that meant. Nor did she have enough interest to ask any more questions. Instead, she let the conversation drift to a halt, sipping her hot chocolate and watching the people at the event.

Children ran about, bundled in stocking caps and

coats to ward off the chilly evening air. Couples huddled together, sharing their drinks and peppermint bark from the food cart. As she watched the crowd, the choir switched songs, transitioning into a beautiful, pensive version of "God Rest Ye Merry Gentlemen."

"I love that song," she said absently after it was finished.

There was no response from the bench next to her and she glanced at Brad, only to find that he had fallen asleep. Alexis pressed her lips together to keep from laughing, shaking her head and burying her head in her hands.

This was really happening. Unbelievable.

Gingerly, she stood, trying not to wake his sleeping form. Across the sidewalk, she spotted Jared walking toward her. She held a finger to her lips to shush him, before he could make any extra noise. Not that the event going on around them was especially quiet right now.

Jared's gaze slid to Brad on the bench, and an amused expression crossed his face. Trying not to laugh, she pulled on Jared's arm, tugging him off to the side of the path, a few yards away from her date.

"What did you do? Bore him to sleep with your rant about the second amendment?"

Alexis laughed. "Hey, nobody gets bored listening to that."

Jared raised his eyebrows.

"Okay, fine. Maybe if you've heard it a time or two."

"Or five or six," he amended.

Somehow, Jared had only been here for thirty seconds, and she was already having more fun than she had had the entire thirty minutes she spent with Brad before he fell asleep.

"Apparently, Brad stayed up all night playing a video game he has played for fifteen years now." She made her eyes wide and nodded solemnly, as though she were impressed with the accomplishment.

Jared made a face. "Oh? That's... responsible."

"Pretty much my thoughts exactly." She rolled her eyes.

The choir shifted into a different song, the melodic chords of "Angels We Have Heard on High" floating above the crowd in a joyous refrain.

"Video games was number three, right? How was number two?"

Alexis rolled her eyes. "Number two took me to Liberty Grille. He sent his steak back twice and made a scene steamrolling the manager into comping the entire date. I don't think I can show my face at the lodge for a year."

She had been horrified at the time, and even the memory was making her anxiety kick up a notch.

"Yikes. So I take it there will be no second date?"

Alexis snorted. "Yeah, not so much. He actually had the gall to try to kiss me good night at my car. I came this close to decking him." She held her thumb and forefinger an inch apart.

Jared released a loud laugh. "I think I would have had to pay Mac to give me the security footage if that had happened."

She shook her head. "It was awful. I just keep thinking, how am I going to survive *seven* more dates? This is torture. I'd rather go through the Crucible all over again." Well, maybe that wasn't entirely true. The intense final challenge of Marine recruit training had been the closest she ever came to quitting during boot camp.

"Oh come on. It's not that bad." Jared nudged her with his shoulder. Leave it to him to call out her dramatics.

"Fine. But it's close."

"Just think, by next year, you'll be able to swear off dates again forever."

There was something in Jared's voice that she couldn't place, but before she could question him about it, Mayor Starling took the stage and started the festivities.

"So who'd you get for your Secret Santa assignment?" Jared whispered the question in her ear.

"I actually got Trudy, the organizer," she answered absently, watching with amusement as children rushed to the tree with their ornaments. The older ones carefully climbed up the stairs to the platforms to put a few of them higher up.

"Oh, that's cool. Do you know her very well?"

Alexis shook her head. "Her list was pretty helpful though. I'm going to start with something from Stories and Scones. Can't go wrong there, right?"

Jared nodded. "That's definitely a safe bet. Maybe I should send myself some Secret Santa gifts," he joked. "I like cookies."

She grinned. "I don't think it works like that. But maybe while I'm grabbing something for Trudy, I'll pick you up some snickerdoodles."

"I knew there was a reason I kept you around," he said with a wink, filling her with flutters she couldn't deny.

Why did her friend have to be so charming and handsome?

She glanced back at her blind date, still snoring on the bench and drawing the laughter of a group of teenagers across the yard.

And why couldn't her actual dates be more like Jared?

JARED HAD IMMEDIATELY KNOWN what he wanted to get Alexis for the first gift. Then he'd questioned himself endlessly about whether it was a good idea or not. And then he spent two hours trying to figure out how to get one on such short notice. Then he remembered his mom had gotten one of those fancy machines that cut vinyl for T-shirts and whatnot.

He sent her the image he'd designed on Sunday. His mom stopped by DK9 to deliver it to him on Monday morning.

He unrolled the large paper and grinned. "This is perfect, Mom. Thanks so much for doing this."

"I wasn't so sure about the design, but I think you're right. Alexis is going to love it. I'm just glad the craft store had enough adhesive vinyl. I thought I was going to have to go to Denver. Tasha really has a good setup over at the Crafter's Corner."

"I'm glad you have a local place now," he said absently as he studied the design.

The decal had a logo of a time bomb on it, with dictionary-style definition.

Se·cur·it·y Spe·cial·ist
/si-kyoor-i-tee spesh-uh-list/
(noun)

1. A career featuring hours of boredom punctuated by moments of sheer terror.
2. Like a normal person but way more impressive. See also: brave, amazing, incredible

HIS PLAN WAS to sneak into her office at Got Your Six and hang up the decal on her office wall. He just needed a little help from someone to make it happen. Luckily, he knew just the person to help him out. It needed to be the last person Alexis would suspect, and the one most likely to withstand her interrogation. So Tessa was definitely out. If she got any hint of Jared being the Secret Santa, Alexis would know in a heartbeat.

After meeting Toby for coffee at Stories and Scones, Jared followed him back to Got Your Six headquarters, parking his car around the corner until he saw Alexis leave on the errand Toby conveniently sent her on when he got back.

Jared pulled toward the back entrance, grabbing the decal and the card he was going to leave along with the gift.

Toby held the back door open. "Well, come on now. She's fixin' to be back in fifteen minutes."

"Is anyone else here?"

Toby shook his head. "Everyone else took the day off after the holiday weekend."

"Awesome, thanks!"

Jared quickly got to work, choosing the wall opposite the door, behind the desk.

He carefully applied the sticker to the wall, using a credit card to get out all of the air bubbles. When he was finished, Jared took a step back and admired his work. It was the perfect addition to her utilitarian office.

He glanced at the clock for the twentieth time. His heart was racing. He was sure she was going to walk in at any moment. He pulled a piece of tape from the desk and attached the envelope to the wall on top of the decal.

With a wave to Toby, Jared hustled back to his car and left the employee parking lot. Just in time, too, because he saw Alexis's car coming back up the street toward the alleyway.

It had been a successful mission, but he did wish he could see her reaction to his gift. He would have to be sure he arranged for her to receive at least one while he was with her. As long as his acting skills were up to the challenge of pretending he didn't know anything about it.

6

Alexis carried in the groceries Toby had sent her out for. She didn't understand why he couldn't have done it himself, but whatever. This way she could be sure to stock the peppermint mocha coffee creamer she preferred this time of year.

"I'm back. You'll never guess what I saw at the grocery store."

Toby lifted the bags from her hands. "What was it?"

"You know about this crazy Secret Santa thing, right? Well, apparently, one of the cashiers is in it. Her Secret Santa had a singing telegram company come from Denver." Initially, Alexis had laughed at the display–a performer in a hippopotamus costume belting out the classic kids song. But the

cashier had been beet red and obviously uncom-
fortable.

"Poor girl. She was so embarrassed. I'm just glad
that particular gift-giver didn't get my name. Bad
enough that Tessa signed me up for this thing
without permission, but if I get publicly embarrassed because of it, I'm never going to let her live it
down."

"Well, cher, I don't think you have to worry about
that."

Toby's knowing smile made her pause her efforts
to load the snacks into the breakroom fridge. "What
do you know?"

"I know nothin'." He shrugged. "But you might go
check out your office."

Alexis narrowed her eyes at him. "Is it filled with
balloons or something?"

Toby laughed in his boisterous, hearty way.
"Nothing like that, cher. Jus' go."

"Fine. But you were in charge of security, and I'm
holding you responsible if my stash of Reese's
Christmas Trees is missing."

Toby shooed her out of the breakroom, and she
headed toward her office, wary of what she was
going to find. She'd finally gotten Tessa to admit
what she'd written on the submission form. Gardening? What a joke.

Turning the corner into her office, Tessa took in

the new decal that spread over the wall. It took up at least four feet of the empty white space. Her smile grew as she read the definitions of security specialist.

"Oh my goodness. This is incredible."

She spotted the pink envelope taped to the wall and eagerly grabbed it. Whoever her Secret Santa was had nailed it with this gift.

The card inside was a simple Christmas notecard with a handwritten note.

DEAR ALEXIS,
I hope you like this addition to your office.
Don't ever forget how special you are!

JOYFULLY YOURS,
Your Secret Santa

SHE COULDN'T HELP but smile at the sweet message. Alexis analyzed the handwriting but couldn't place it. It was feminine, that was for sure. The letters were round and loopy. The kind of handwriting she'd always admired but never been able to achieve. Her own looked more like a serial killer's scrawl than she'd rather admit, based on her expert opinion from binge-watching ten seasons of *Criminal Minds*.

Could it be Tessa? She would have access to her office and was thoughtful enough to do something so personal, like the decal. Tessa had been bugging Alexis to add something decorative to her office since she started working at Got Your Six a couple of years ago, although mostly she'd focused her efforts on breaking through Adam's gruff demeanor. Quite successfully, based on how the relationship had developed.

But the handwriting didn't look like Tessa's, either.

Which left... someone else. Who apparently knew her fairly well. Maybe this whole Secret Santa thing wouldn't be such a terrible experience. She was going to have fun buying gifts for Trudy, and if her Secret Santa kept spoiling her like this, it would almost make up for the seven additional dates she still needed to go on.

"Whatd'ya think?"

Toby was in her doorway, leaning on the frame with his arms crossed.

"It's pretty cool, right?"

He nodded. "I think I want one for my office, actually."

"So who is it?"

Toby smiled and shook his head. "I don't know what you mean. I didn't see anything."

She narrowed her eyes at him. "Liar." She looked back at her wall with a smile. "But that's okay. Maybe it's more fun not to know."

"You ready for your next date?"

Alexis sagged. "Please don't make me. I'll do anything, seriously."

Toby grinned. "Not a chance. You know I can't let you out of it. A bet is a bet. Besides, I really think this one is a keeper."

"Who is it this time?"

"Tessa suggested him."

Alexis groaned. "Seriously? Is it Jared?"

Toby raised a single eyebrow. "I wouldn't think that would be so bad. But no. It's Connor. He's a firefighter."

Alexis remembered the nice single dad from a Christmas Eve gathering at Jan's house a few years back. "Oh," she said. That actually didn't sound terrible. "What are we doing?"

"Tessa agreed to babysit his son so you two could grab dinner."

"How nice of her," Alexis deadpanned.

"Be nice, Alexis."

She made a face at him, but softened. She knew her friend had good intentions. It wasn't Tessa's fault that Alexis was never going to be with anyone. Or Toby's, for that matter.

She just had to get through these dates and that would be the end of it. Connor was nice enough, but even if she would consider dating, she definitely wasn't equipped to be a mother.

She snapped a picture of her wall and sent it to Tessa.

Alexis: My Secret Santa has set the bar pretty high.

Tessa: What?! That's amazing. Who is it?

Alexis: I'm not sure yet. Handwriting says it's a woman.

Tessa: Interesting… I got a gift card for a manicure. Want to come with me?

Alexis glanced down at her stubby fingernails, the unfortunate victim of her anxiety-induced nail-biting habit.

Alexis: I'll pass. I bet Claire would go.

She sent the photo to Jared, too.

Jared: Cool! Where'd you get it? Something like that would look cool at DK9.

Alexis: My Secret Santa.

Jared: Nice. That beats a cheap ornament, I suppose.

He didn't say anything more, and Alexis slid her phone back in her bag. She needed to get back to work on the proposal for Chris Tooley and his new partners in the consulting firm they'd established.

Apparently, they dealt with some pretty highly classified material and wanted to make sure their new office in Freedom was properly secured.

Her eyes kept drifting back to the fun and stylish wall to her right. Regardless of what she told Toby, she was dying to know who had given her such an extravagant gift that was perfect for her.

JARED REREAD THE TEXT EXCHANGE, wishing he could see Alexis's emotions behind the words. She'd sent the photo, which he assumed meant she liked it... but now he was reading the messages and overanalyzing that she didn't actually say that.

All she'd said was that it was from her Secret Santa. He'd said everything else, even commenting about getting one for DK9 to throw her off the trail.

With a groan, he tossed his phone onto the desk and turned back to his computer. His research about non-profits was overwhelming, but he felt like he was starting to get a handle on it.

Kyle and his daughter were coming this week just to meet Ruby and do the initial paperwork. Then they would come again in January to do their two-week onsite handler training. Between those appointments, he would be helping make sure Ruby was completely honed in on peanut detection. He'd ordered peanut powder, which he could dilute to allow the dog to practice accurate detections on fractional parts per billion concentrations once they got down to those levels.

He glanced at the training schedule he'd drawn up and then went to get Ruby from the pen. He spent the afternoon building Ruby's association between the peanut smell and all the positive reinforcement of treats, praise, and play. She was already an incredibly well-behaved dog, and she was at the perfect stage to introduce her specialized skill set.

While Derek preferred to focus on search and rescue and bomb or drug dogs, Jared liked the science and potential of the dogs for service applications. They didn't do guide dogs for the visually impaired at DK9, but if it involved the dog's nose? It fell in their scope. And Derek had been great about letting Jared broaden their application base with the stroke-detection, blood sugar level alerts, and the allergy detection dogs.

He put Ruby back in her pen after their session, and his gaze slid toward Maverick. The sweet golden lab had failed another test at Pete's cabin. They'd work with him for another two weeks before retesting. If he failed again, he would officially be out of the running as a search and rescue dog.

Then they would adopt him out, but Jared wasn't quite ready to say good-bye.

Maybe Alexis would adopt him. He'd been trying to convince her to get a dog for the last year. She might insist that everything was fine, but she seemed lonely.

He'd give it a few weeks, but if Maverick wasn't cut out to be a SAR dog, Jared thought he'd make the perfect dog for Alexis. If he couldn't convince her to be with him, maybe he could at least convince her to embrace another kind of companion.

He had a few other dogs to work with this afternoon before it was time to head to his men's Bible study group. The men's group was where Jared connected with most of his friends in Freedom. Even though Jared had grown up here, most of his friends came from church rather than surviving the decade since high school.

That evening, he grabbed his Bible from the passenger seat of his truck and headed inside, catching up with Pete O'Roarke as they crossed the parking lot. Pete was married to Jan, who owned Stories and Scones, and seemed to know everyone in town.

"How are you doing, Jared?"

"Can't complain, sir. How about you?"

Pete's smile was wide. "It's the best time of the year, don't you know?"

They made their way into the large conference room where the Bible study was held. Jared waved to

Aiden, Ty, and Derek, who had already claimed seats near the food.

Pastor Stephenson held up his arms and spoke loudly to get everyone's attention, causing Jared to scramble for the nearest seat, which put him next to James Pruitt, an older man who mostly stayed quiet. He smiled and looked back toward Pastor Stephenson.

"All right, gentlemen, before we get started, I have a few announcements. Shayla has asked me to remind everyone that the Christmas caroling outing is in two weeks on Wednesday."

Good-natured groans echoed through the room. Jared could understand why. Most guys didn't exactly dream of walking around in the cold singing Christmas songs.

It wasn't his first choice either. Thankfully, he hadn't been dragged along since he was in high school. Once, he'd actually asked Melody if she wanted to go. She'd laughed for twenty minutes. But the truth was, he wouldn't mind doing something like that—with the right person.

"Now, now. Come on," Pastor Stephenson admonished. This year, we're caroling at the local assisted living center, instead of traipsing through the snow from house to house."

"So quit your griping and spread some Christmas cheer!"

Laughter erupted at Pete's good-natured addition to the announcement.

Pastor Stephenson chuckled. "Yes, well. What he said. Oh, the only other announcement I have is that this is our last meeting for the year. I'll see you after the New Year when we'll start our study on the book of 1 Timothy."

Jared made a mental note to change his calendar for the next couple of weeks. They always took a break around the holidays, but he missed the camaraderie that came with this tight-knit group of men gathering over the Word. The group of high school boys he led would take a break for the holidays, too.

He was going to have to go caroling just to fill up his time.

Maybe he could convince Alexis to go with him. The idea made him laugh out loud, before he realized Pastor Stephenson was in the middle of praying over the study they were about to do. He quickly silenced himself and refocused his heart and mind. If this was the last study before Christmas, he was determined to get his mind off Alexis while he drank in the wisdom of the Word.

7

---

*B*owling wasn't exactly Alexis's first choice for activities, but it wasn't the most awkward date she'd ever been on.

She released the ball toward the pins, staying to watch it veer to the right just as it reached the pins. Five pins. Oh well, that was better than the gutter ball she'd gotten last frame. When she turned, Connor was clapping his hands and smiling at her.

That was the part of bowling she didn't like—everyone watching you every single turn. At least if you were hiking or skating, everyone was mostly too preoccupied with their own actions to worry about anyone else. But bowling? It was like being on stage.

She gave a tight smile. "Getting better, right?"

Connor held his hand up for a high five. "Defi-

TARA GRACE ERICSON

nitely. Before long, you'll be on the wall of fame over there in a pink bowling shirt."

Despite herself, Alexis laughed at his teasing. "Not likely."

She took her seat and grabbed a few nachos while watching Connor throw a strike. She shook her head as he moonwalked backward then spun around on his heel with his hands extended, waving his fingers in what Tessa would call jazz hands.

She clapped good-naturedly. He sat across from her at the little table.

"So, are *you* on the wall of fame over there in a pink bowling shirt?"

Connor laughed. "Maybe someday. I don't exactly have a lot of free time right now. Between Luke and the station, I barely have time to myself."

"That must be really hard. Being a parent seems intimidating enough, but on your own?"

He shrugged. "It is and it isn't, you know? You just… do what you gotta do each day. And then you try to sleep and do it over again. Letting Luke down isn't an option. Same for the fire station."

Alexis nodded. She could understand that. It was a lot like how she had functioned in the Marines toward the end. And sometimes how she operated now. One day at a time.

"Don't you get tired of being in survival mode?"

"Some days feel like that. Other days? It's a really

70

good life. Luke is the coolest little kid. And I get to do a job I love." He shrugged. "It seems silly to complain."

Alexis didn't know how to respond to that, so she stood up and took her turn while mulling over his words.

She was tired of living in survival mode. And the thing was, she wasn't sure she needed to be. Her job was, as the new decorations in her office perfectly explained, mostly low-key. Absently, she grabbed the ball from the return and sent it toward the end of the lane again.

She had enough money. Good friends. A God who loved her.

Yet she lived in a state of tension she couldn't seem to explain. Even with the help of her medication. She didn't let herself rest. Or dream. Or plan.

A crash of pins followed by loud cheering to her left jolted her out of her reverie. She turned and saw Jared receiving high fives from a small group of high school boys.

She smiled, watching him redirect the attention from himself and toward the next bowler.

"Nice!"

The voice next to her made her jump. Connor was grinning, and Alexis looked around, trying to figure out what she'd missed.

"That was your first spare, right?" he said,

pointing to the end of the lane where the pins were being reset.

Her eyes tracked back to Jared and found him watching her. She held up a hand, and he gave her a nod. His eyes flicked to Connor, just over her shoulder. Alexis tried to read the expression in her friend's eyes but couldn't. Something was just 'off' with the picture, but she couldn't figure it out. Jared didn't look like himself.

"I think that deserves some ice cream. What do you think?" Connor was an excellent date. Alexis nodded and followed him back to the concession stand. He made her laugh with a story about his son's first time bowling and how he'd gotten stranded in the middle of the lane, unable to walk back due to the wax.

Alexis tried to keep her focus on Connor, but she found herself looking back toward Jared's lane, where he had reengaged with his high schoolers. She watched him joke around with the young men, though his smile seemed slightly forced. Then she realized what had seemed so odd with their interaction earlier.

As often as she saw him, in all kinds of places and times, Jared *always* greeted her with a smile. But tonight, there was no trace of his usual playful demeanor as their eyes met across the bowling alley. Had something happened? Maybe with his brother?

She was determined to figure out what was wrong.

"One ice-cream sundae, extra caramel." He held out the bowl to her.

"Thank you, sir."

She went back to the lane with Connor and they finished up their ice cream and their game of bowling.

"Thanks for meeting up with me tonight. It's been a long time since I've been on a date. I'm glad Toby suggested it."

Alexis smiled at the mention of her friend. "Toby's a good guy, isn't he?"

Connor nodded. "He is. I think he knew I needed a push. After Felicia died, I sort of retreated into my own little world. Even though I don't think you and I are a long-term match, it was really nice to spend time with another adult."

She laughed. "That's a pretty low bar for companionship. Is she an adult? Check."

Flustered, Connor tried to back track his statement, but she waved him off. "No, no. I knew what you meant. I agree. It was fun, and definitely my best blind date so far—another low bar," she added with a funny look, "but I'm not looking for anything more."

He nodded. "Same here. But I think Toby knew this was an important step for me to realize that maybe it was possible and that I deserve to love again. Someday. Down the road, you know?"

Maybe that was what Toby was trying to do with her too. The lovable brat.

After her date left, Alexis wandered down the royal-blue carpet of questionable design and cleanliness toward the lane where Jared and his high school boys were wrapping up their game.

She hung back until Jared looked up from his shoes and spotted her.

"Have a good night, fellas. You've all got my number if you need me over the holidays, right?"

The boys said good-bye and traipsed toward the exit, pushing and teasing one another good-naturedly. Alexis watched as Jared surveyed the now-empty chairs and table and began stacking up cups and trash.

She came down the few steps into the designated seating area to help.

"Hey there," she said, feeling awkward.

"Hey."

He hadn't looked at her yet, his focus on the table.

She waited.

Finally, when there was no more to do, Jared looked at her, his expression pained.

"What's going on? You seem... upset."

His eyes fell shut and he exhaled. "I'm not."

She gave him a look. "Don't lie to me. You're not that good at it," she teased.

He collapsed into one of the seats along the half wall that separated them from another empty lane. "I'm fine. Really. Just tired."

She sat next to him, their legs touching. She didn't say anything until he turned his face to look at her. "Really?" she asked.

JARED STUDIED HER FACE, seeing her genuine concern and friendship in her eyes. She waited for his response, her eyebrows lifted and her smile soft. It was a face he was tempted to spill his soul to. How much could he tell her without scaring her away?

"I just… I didn't realize you were going on a date with Connor."

Alexis's expression changed to one of surprise. "Oh? It was just another one of Toby's grand plans. We had a really good time though."

Her words sliced through him, but he tried not to react. That was exactly what he'd been afraid of.

Sleeping Beauty at the tree lighting or the sniffling sneezer at dinner, he could handle. How was he supposed to compete with a firefighter widower, who happened to be single dad with an adorable kid? Worst of all, he knew Connor was a genuinely good guy. Jared liked him.

Which meant, right now, Jared wanted to slash his tires for taking Alexis on a date. A really good time, to use her words.

"I'm glad you had fun," he forced out with a tight smile.

Alexis laughed, the bright sound a searing contradiction to his foul mood. "No you're not, but that's okay. I'm not interested in him."

"You're not?"

She shook her head. "No. But I think Toby is trying to teach me that maybe it would be okay to open up to the idea of being with someone."

Jared felt the rays of light break through his gray mood. "And how do you feel about that lesson?" He asked the question casually, as though his entire world didn't hinge on her answer.

She shrugged. "I don't know yet. Maybe someday. With the right guy? Maybe."

He wanted to grab her by the shoulders and tell her that *he* was the right guy. Why couldn't she see it? He already knew he cared about Alexis more than she cared about him. No use in scaring her away by getting intense too quickly. Instead, he acted nonchalant. "That's a healthy perspective, I think."

"I still have six dates left, so we'll see. Maybe

Toby is being more strategic about this than I gave him credit for."

Jared grunted in response. Six more dates. He needed to have a talk with Toby about these dates. If he was going to have a chance to convince Alexis that he was the one for her, he was going to need her to have fewer blind dates with great guys like Connor.

Not that he wanted her to be miserable on her dates... but he definitely didn't want her to have any more "great times" on dates unless they were with him.

And he needed to really figure out how to leverage this Secret Santa thing. He had three more gifts to take Alexis from friend to forever. That was a lofty calling for a few Christmas gifts.

8

_____

*A*lexis dropped her bag to the ground in her office with a thud and collapsed in her chair, staring up at the ceiling. She was exhausted.

Who in their right mind thought that skiing on a Tuesday night made for a good date? She loved the slopes as much as the next Freedom resident, but after a full day of work and another ahead of her? She would have much rather grabbed a cup of coffee and a treat from Stories and Scones.

As it was, she'd barely talked to Nick. She took her sweet time going down the runs, despite only the easier runs being open for the late-night ski session. With their conversations limited to rides up the chair lift, the date was painless enough. Other than the tumble she'd taken when remembering how to slow herself down.

Date number five was officially in the books. And she was beginning to rethink her kind thoughts about Toby. He was just messing with her, after all. Or maybe she was just in a bad mood from exhaustion and sore muscles. Plus, it had been eight days and her Secret Santa had gone radio silent.

She knew it was four gifts over the month, but every time she saw her office wall, she got excited about what would come next. But there had been nothing. She'd asked Jared to come help her pick out gifts for Trudy yesterday, but he was busy with his new training client, the girl with the peanut allergy.

She rocked back and pressed forward to force herself out of the chair, all of her muscles protesting after the late-night skiing. She hobbled down the hall to Tessa's office.

"Do you have any painkillers?" she said by way of greeting.

Tessa raised her eyebrows but wordlessly reached into her desk and tossed her a bottle.

"Blessings on you and your household," Alexis said dramatically.

Tessa snorted. "Yeah, okay, Gandalf."

Alexis downed a few pills with her coffee and then leaned back in the chair.

"What's got you all moany this morning?"

Alexis rolled her eyes. "Number five decided late-night skiing at the Ridge was a good date idea."

Tessa tried, unsuccessfully, to hide her laughter. "Oh my, I'm so sorry."

"It's fine. I'm fine. I'm just tired and grumpy."

"Ooh, look what I got from my Secret Santa yesterday." Tessa reached into her bag and pulled out a notebook.

Alexis read the front of it. "Succ it up." The picture on the cover was a small cactus, just like the four or five Tessa had scattered around her office in various mugs and pots. "Nice," she added.

"I know! I just love it. I put that I liked plants on my description. I wonder if that's where they got the idea?"

Alexis shrugged. "No idea."

"What did you get from yours this week?"

"Nothing yet. But it's fine. It's just a dumb gift exchange."

Tessa glared at her. "Lighten up, grumpy gills. You're killing my morning mood."

Alexis made a face and stood up. "Fine. I'll go. But you owe me a present if my Secret Santa drops the ball!" she finished the words from the hallway as she left her friend's office, her mood already brightened just from being with Tessa.

When she got back to her office, Alexis stopped short, her mouth open. "What on earth?"

She'd just left her office not ten minutes ago, but

now there was a huge bouquet of flowers on her desk.

She frowned at the vase as she stepped around her desk, mentally cringing at how much the red and white roses and lilies had likely cost. They were pretty, sure. But they'd die before Christmas.

She tugged the card out of the clip and opened it.

Dear Alexis,

Cookies are made to be enjoyed and appreciated for a short time.

And so are flowers.

But since you can't eat these, I chose ones that would last forever, which is how long you deserve to be loved by someone special.

Thoughtfully Yours,

Your Secret Santa

Alexis puzzled at the message until she looked at the flower arrangement. What she'd assumed were real flowers were actually very convincing fakes. She lifted up the vase and tipped it side to side, smiling when the 'water' didn't move. It was fake, too!

She hadn't seen it before, but now that she held the vase of fake blooms, she saw the box tucked next to it. The Stories and Scones logo–along with the message on the card–gave her a hint at what waited inside.

The pumpkin snickerdoodles were nested neatly in tissue paper, individually wrapped in clear plastic sleeves. Her favorite.

She moved her flowers to the top of the filing cabinet across the room and sat back at her desk. Unwrapping one of the cookies, despite the early hour, she reread the note.

Warmth spread through her center as she soaked in the words. How did this stranger know exactly what she needed to hear? And exactly what to get her!

Tessa had given her a cactus last year and despite her assurances that they were incredibly easy to take care of, it had died by March. Fake flowers were the only kind Alexis needed to be entrusted with. And she'd never seen ones as convincing as these.

But the note had touched another nerve. One that had been bouncing around in her head since her date with Connor.

He'd said he deserved to be loved.

And Alexis wasn't sure she felt that way. Sure, she believed Jesus loved her. She even believed Jesus could handle her brokenness. But asking someone else to deal with the anxiety and depression that followed her around was too much. Wasn't it?

Her Secret Santa didn't seem to think so.

But they didn't know her. Or, at least, she didn't think they did.

She only knew a few people who had signed up for the exchange. If she hadn't literally been sitting in Tessa's office while this was delivered, she would think it was from her friend.

Maybe she recruited help.

"Tessa? Are you my Secret Santa?" she yelled the question, sure that her voice would carry through the small office.

Instead of an answer, hurried footsteps echoed down the hall. "What did you get?" came Tessa's breathless question.

Alexis stared at her friend, trying to decipher any hint of deception. "You tell me."

Tessa rolled her eyes. "I already told you, I'm not your Secret Santa." Then, Tessa's eyes found the flowers and she went all soft and gooey. "Oh my word, they're beautiful!"

She stepped toward the arrangement and felt one of the petals. She gasped. "They're fake? Oh my word, that's brilliant."

Alexis sighed. "Isn't it, though? Are you sure it wasn't you?"

"Girl, I wish I could take credit for this because that's amazing. But no."

"And you don't know who it is?"

Tessa shook her head.

Alexis held out the card. "Here, read this."

Tessa scanned the letter and then squealed. "That's so sweet."

"Is it? Or is it weird? Like, why are they telling me I deserve to be loved?"

Tessa raised her eyebrows. "Umm, because you do? And because everyone close to you can see that you don't believe it."

Alexis frowned. "Really?" Tessa just nodded. "How can anyone say that, though? It isn't like God owes me a marriage or a life with someone else. Paul writes a whole bunch about it. People can be single and content, okay?"

Tessa crossed her arms. "Are you single and content? Or are you hiding from the idea of a future with someone because you don't think someone would want to be with you?"

Alexis swallowed her immediate rejection of Tessa's words. Because as much as she wanted to defend her stance—the one she'd developed for years about how she was meant to be single and would embrace it—the truth was far different.

She hadn't embraced it, had she.

She'd just been in survival mode.

Tessa gently set the letter back on the desk. "I don't know who your Secret Santa is. But you should listen to them."

JARED WENT to Stories and Scones later that day. Apparently, Alexis was feeling the pressure to get Trudy something special, and Tessa was tied up and couldn't help.

Alexis was leaning on the glass window by the door when he arrived. She straightened up and tucked her phone into her pocket. "Hey, stranger."

He grinned. "Hey." He hadn't seen Alexis since the bowling alley, and that hadn't exactly been a shining moment for him. His immediate jealousy at watching her with Connor had been a bit over the top. But hearing that Alexis was softening to the idea of dating had made him optimistic, and a little more daring with his latest Secret Santa gift.

"I thought we'd grab a drink and then we can check a few shops for gifts for Trudy?"

"Sounds good to me. Why the rush?"

She waved him toward the line and they took their place. "I'm just seeing what everyone else is getting for their gifts and feeling like I should probably step it up a bit for Trudy, you know? She's the brains behind this whole thing."

"So people have been getting good stuff?" he prodded. He was hoping she'd say something about the gifts she'd received. His own Secret Santa had done all right with some pumpkin snickerdoodles and a "Man's Best Friend" picture frame. Eventually, Jared would get around to printing a photo of him and Chewy, his own dog, to put inside it.

Or that was what he was telling himself. In all likelihood, it would be next Christmas before he got it done.

Alexis nodded, her eyes wide. "Oh yeah. Tessa got a cute notebook that's perfect for her. And someone got Megan Held a waterproof notepad so she can write down story ideas in the shower. How brilliant is that for an author?"

"Huh. That is cool. I didn't even know that existed. Maybe I need one of those for my crazy shower ideas," he said. "What about you? Anything good?"

"Well, I showed you the wall sticker, right?"

"Oh yeah, you did." He pretended to remember, as though he hadn't painstakingly applied every inch of the large decoration. "And you were happy with it?"

Her eyes brightened. "Oh yeah, it's super cool. And this week, they gave me a bouquet of flowers and some of Jan's cookies."

"Flowers? Don't you hate flowers?" Jared felt a

twinge of guilt, acting like he didn't know the answer to the question.

"Usually," Alexis answered, "but these were fake! I can't shake the idea that it is someone who knows me really well. Because honestly, who gives fake flowers? And the note was..." She sighed with a soft smile as she trailed off.

He nudged her with his shoulder. "Earth to Alex! The note?"

A touch of pink flooded her cheeks, and it was everything Jared could do not to brush her face with his hand.

"It was just a nice note." She cleared her throat. "Anyway, it's all making me feel like I need to do a little better for Trudy. It's not like my gift-giving list is out of control this year. I can afford to splurge to make her holiday a bit brighter."

"That's nice. I got the feeling she's a bit lonely this time of year."

"Oh? I didn't realize you knew Trudy."

Jared coughed. "Oh, yeah. You know," he scrambled for something to say, "small town and all that."

"Next!"

Incredibly grateful for the interruption, Jared stepped forward with a smile at Jan. If anyone could be called a staple of Freedom, Colorado, it was Jan Clark, now Jan O'Rourke. With her warm, inviting personality and her place as Freedom's favorite coffee shop owner, everyone in town knew Jan. More impressively, Jan knew and cared for everyone in town.

"Good morning, Jared. Alexis, it's so good to see you!"

"Hey, how are things going?" he asked.

Jan laughed merrily. "It is great, but busy. I had to bring on another baker. I think everyone in town is buying sweets for their Secret Santas."

Jared grinned. "It's a pretty safe bet, I would say."

Alexis chimed in, "My Secret Santa gave some to me."

Jan's eyes twinkled. Jared fidgeted nervously. Jan couldn't possibly know that the cookies he bought on Monday were for Alexis. Surely, he was just one of hundreds of customers Jan had each day.

"Well, isn't that lovely. What can I get for you today?"

"I will take a Ridgetop mocha, and I'm guessing Alexis wants a salted caramel latte." He turned to Alexis and waited for her approval. She nodded and he smiled. He loved that he knew her well enough to guess her order.

"Coming right up. What are you two up to today?" Jan asked as she rang up the orders.

"Doing some shopping for my role as a Secret Santa," Alexis explained. "What better way to spoil someone than to find something fun and unique from one of Freedom's local businesses?"

Jan grinned. "That's just wonderful. I think many other Santas have had the same idea. Trudy is just doing a wonderful job with this whole event, isn't she?"

"Definitely," Alexis agreed.

When their drinks were ready, Jared pointed to the books at the back of the store. "What about a book for Trudy?"

Alexis shook her head. "There was nothing in her bio about her being a reader. I wouldn't even know where to begin. Let's just take a walk around the square and check out some of the other shops."

A few minutes later, they approached Wick and Sarcasm, a local candle shop located across the square from Stories and Scones. Jared had never actually been inside, though he saw the candles around his mom's house all the time.

"Would a candle be a copout?" Alexis asked.

Jared shrugged. "I don't think so. If people will use them, then it's a good gift that doesn't become clutter."

Alexis shrugged. "Come on, let's check it out."

The scent inside the store hit his nose as they opened the door. It wasn't quite like walking past the store in the mall in Denver where the overwhelming body wash and hand soap assaulted your senses, even from outside the opening.

The candle store smelled Christmasy, like spiced apple cider and cranberries.

Alexis took a deep inhale and sighed. "Oh my, that's amazing."

Jared had to agree. He wasn't really the kind of person who thought to light a candle at his house or office, but if his house could smell like this, then maybe he'd be converted.

"Hey there. How can I help you?"

"We're just browsing," Jared replied.

"Great!" the shopkeeper said cheerily. "We've got all of our autumn scents 30% off, and our new Christmas collection is right over there. The one we're burning today is called Cozy Christmas Cabin. Let me know if you need any help."

"Thank you," Alexis said softly. She was already browsing the shelves, lifting glass containers to her nose.

He saw her nose wrinkle as she pulled one away. Why was she so darn cute?

"Not a fan?"

She shook her head. "I'm just not a fan of floral scents."

He scanned the label. "Honeysuckle and apple," he read aloud. He raised it to his nose and tipped his head in response. It was summery and fresh. He kind of liked it. But he supposed everyone's nose was just as different as their taste buds. What would Alexis like?

"I wonder what Trudy would like?" he mused instead.

"Let's try out the Christmas section. I think if I get one of the bigger candles and maybe pair it with some Christmas earrings from Jessica, it would make a nice gift.

"Who's Jessica?"

"Oh, she's in my women's study group at church. She has a little online boutique where she sells earrings and bookmarks. If I wore earrings, I would totally wear hers."

He glanced at her ears. "I'm not sure I ever realized you didn't have your ears pierced."

"Maybe there is a lot you don't know about me," she said with a wink.

He smiled in response. "Maybe so. I have a feeling I could spend my entire life learning all your twists and turns and I wouldn't get bored."

As soon as the admission was out of his mouth, he prayed he hadn't gone too far. Alexis simply smiled and pulled one of the Christmas candles from the shelf to smell.

"What do you think of this one?" she asked.

The candle was labeled "Freedom Frost" and had a nice fresh, minty scent. "Ooh, I like that a lot." He grabbed another. It smelled like cinnamon rolls and reminded him of early mornings at Stories and Scones.

He wandered away from Alexis and looked over the shelves stocked with all kinds of candles. A sign caught his eye.

We make custom candles on request. Ask a store associate for details.

He filed away the information and continued browsing. He'd have to come back without Alexis to make it work. But the ideas were rolling around his mind as he read candle labels and smelled the various concoctions Ashley dreamed up.

Alexis appeared next to him, a large glass jar candle in hand. "I'm going to go with this Cozy Christmas Cabin one. It just smelled so good when we walked in."

Jared smiled. "Sounds perfect. I'm sure Trudy will love it."

Alexis chewed her lip. "Do you think so?"

"I do. If nothing else, she can burn it at her Open Houses to make the house super inviting. Even when it isn't Christmastime."

"That's a good point," Alexis said. "Okay. I'm sold. I'll get this and some of Jessica's new Christmas earrings." She exhaled. "I'm good. At least until the next week."

Jared smiled. "It'll be great. I don't think this is

about the particular gifts for Trudy. She just wants everyone to have a chance to have the thrill of a little gift, the joy of giving to someone else, and to bring the community of Freedom together. It's not about what you give her."

Alexis sighed. "You're right. Thank you. But I still think she'll love this. And maybe we can go check out Tuck's shop. He has the most incredible hand-made cutting boards."

Jared held out his elbow for her to grab and put on his best high-society accent. "I'd be positively honored to accompany you, miss."

Alexis rolled her eyes with a smile, but she grabbed his elbow with her hand, walking close to his side as they went to the back of the shop to pay for her candle.

At Tuck's woodworking shop, Jared bought one of the cutting boards, which Alexis's raving description hadn't undersold in the least. It would be a great gift for his parents. For his brother, he bought a wooden boot jack. He figured it was a small convenience that his rugged cowboy brother probably didn't have but might actually use. And this one had the Denver Broncos logo on it, which would make it hard for Jason to throw away.

"Do you want to grab lunch? We could make up for your blind date and have El Cresta?"

When it looked like Alexis was going to decline

the invitation, Jared put on his best puppy-dog pleading face. "Don't say you're going to make me eat alone, Alex. Pretty please?"

Alexis burst into laughter and shook her head. "You're incorrigible, you know that?"

He grinned. "I know. But you like it."

"Fine. Lunch sounds good. But you have to make sure we only eat one basket of chips. Last time I was here—Stuffy McSneezerson not included—I didn't even get to enjoy my tamales because I was so full on chips and salsa."

Jared put his hands on his hips and pushed out his chest in a Superman pose. "Have no fear, young maiden. I solemnly swear to bogart the chips so you don't ruin your appetite."

Alexis laughed again, and Jared dropped the pose, the smile on his face spreading even wider.

He knew it was pathetic, but her laughter was by far the best gift he could ask for.

ALEXIS REACHED across the table for another chip. Jared pulled the basket out of her reach.

"My precious," he said in a creepy tone.

She wriggled her shoulders in disgust. "Oh my. Ew. Please don't ever do that again."

"Come on, what? You like *Lord of the Rings*."

"But I don't like Gollum. He's so creepy." She glared at him. "And give me a chip."

"You said not to!" He slid the basket toward her though.

"Yeah, well…" Hmm, she had said that, hadn't she? "We haven't eaten the whole basket yet."

Jared raised his eyebrows and looked down at the basket of chips. She followed his gaze and saw what caused his reaction. The white paper sat nearly empty, just one lonely, broken chip remaining in the bottom.

"Go ahead. You're right. We haven't eaten the *entire* basket," Jared said sarcastically.

She made a face at him but grabbed the chip anyway. El Cresta was busy for lunch, as usual. But she didn't mind waiting. Especially not with Jared. She hadn't laughed as much as she had this morning in a long time.

And it was all thanks to him.

"Thank you," she said, her tone serious.

Jared quirked a smile. "It's just a chip," he said.

Her lips twitched, but she shook her head. "No, not that. Just… for coming today. For being my friend. I know I'm not easy sometimes."

Jared reached across the table and touched her fingers. "Hey now, what is that supposed to mean?"

Alexis lifted one shoulder. "I'm just grateful for you, I suppose. You and Tessa… I feel like I don't deserve you guys. I always feel a bit like the dark cloud on your otherwise bright days." She looked up from their intertwined fingers. His eyes were kindly questioning her, and she felt her stomach flip under his scrutiny.

Jared squeezed her fingers tightly for a moment. He ducked slightly, drawing even closer across the table. "You know we love you, right?"

She nodded, the lump in her throat tightening further.

"And you know you don't have to pretend for us?" His words were soft and gentle, and they soothed a part of her soul she hadn't even known was scraped and tender. He continued, his words low, almost disappearing amidst the rambunctious noise of the bustling restaurant around them. "I don't want you to ever feel like you have to put on a mask for me, Alexis. It would break my heart to know that you felt like you couldn't be your whole self."

She pressed her lips together and nodded again. "Yeah, I know," she choked out.

She looked away, unable to take the intensity of emotion she saw in his eyes. She tugged her fingers free and glanced around the restaurant, willing away the stinging of tears behind her eyes. Why had she even said anything?

Jared must have sensed she needed a change of

subject because he leaned back. "So, what are you getting me for Christmas? I've been very good this year, you know." His voice was full of mischief and teasing, and a smile tugged at her lips, despite the heaviness of the previous moments.

"Somehow, I doubt that. You're trouble, Jared Keen."

His crooked grin was accompanied by an eyebrow raise. "Oh, I don't know. I wouldn't call it trouble."

"And what would you call it?"

He opened his arms to the side. "Hmm. Boyish charm? Entertainment? Good-natured mischief? Take your pick. It's hard to go wrong, am I right?"

She laughed. "Yeah, you're right."

The server brought their food and set it in front of them.

"Mind if I pray?" Jared asked, extending his hand across the table to her.

She grabbed it, reforging the connection their fingers had before she tugged hers away earlier. She listened to his prayer, his strong words clear and genuine. A hint of laughter in them, even as he talked to the Lord about their friendship and time together. Had she ever laughed during prayer?

He finished, a final touching expression of thanks for her that had the tears refilling in her eyes. Jared might be sunshine, full of laughter and joy that made her ache for the ability to chase away her own ever-present sadness. but there was no doubt in her mind that he was also solid, built on a foundation that would stand when the rains came.

Rain was one thing. The hurricane of her issues was another.

And to cast darkness into his life seemed almost cruel.

But she couldn't stay away. She needed him too much. She needed his friendship.

She couldn't let herself entertain the idea of needing him more.

Even if she would happily spend every Saturday morning the way they had today.

Date number six had been last night—a perfectly boring evening at the fundraising dance. It was fine. But it was also another reminder that not all men or relationships were created equal. The entire time she was there with Logan, she couldn't help but think how much more fun the evening would have been if it had been Jared on her arm instead.

Jared cared about her so deeply, it was almost irresistible to give in to the desire to let him try to love away her shadows. It was a foolish thought though. She knew enough about PTSD to know that no one could love it away.

While she prayed to the Lord for healing, until that day or until the other side of heaven, she knew this was just a fight she was in for the long haul. And she'd come to terms with fighting it alone.

But Jared…

He made her question whether she really had to do it alone.

And with her Secret Santa, whoever they were, leaving cryptic notes of encouragement? Maybe God was trying to tell her something as well.

9

*J*ared went back to Wick and Sarcasm on Monday morning, when he knew Alexis would be back at work.

"Hello," a friendly woman with Felicity handwritten on her nametag greeted him. "Welcome to Wick and Sarcasm. How can I help you?"

"I had a question about the custom candles."

"Oh! Well, I'm pretty new here, but ask away, and if I can't find the answer, we'll track down Ashley from the back room."

"How does it work? I have someone in mind, but I have no idea how to pick the smells or anything."

Felicity smiled broadly. "Sure thing. What we do is bring you into the back room and talk through the options for scents. We'll mix it up right there and pour the candle. Then we'll print the label later today, and you can come pick up the candle tomorrow."

Jared sighed in relief. "Oh that's awesome. I was afraid it would be like two weeks."

"Well, I think usually we require appointments for people to come in and make their candles, but there's no one on the schedule this morning. So if you want, we can go see if Ashley has time."

"Let's do it."

Felicity led Jared through an area marked "Employees Only." He was amazed by the space, with silver stock pots, hundreds of empty glass and tin jars, and rows of little vials.

A short woman was sitting at a computer, her back to him. When she whirled around, he saw the familiar face of Ashley Johnson. He knew her and her family from church.

"Jared! What brings you in today?"

Felicity beamed. "He wants to make a custom candle for *someone special*." The musical lilt she put on the final words made heat rise in his cheeks.

Ashley grinned. "Is that right? Well, let me get you the questionnaire and order form. You can fill it out while I just finish this set of labels."

She rifled through a stack of papers on the desk and handed one to him, along with a pen.

"Have a seat anywhere you can find one. Feel free to look at the fragrance oils for inspiration, but please don't open any. I can help you do that whenever we get to the actual decision-making."

Felicity went back out to the front of the shop, leaving Jared and Ashley in the workroom. He filled out the order form, noting the price was more than the candles out front, but not unreasonable for the specialized time and attention.

There was a section at the end of the form where it asked him to list a few scents he wanted for the candle. It even suggested listing characteristics of the person it was intended for. He remembered some of the candles he'd looked at on Saturday, then he scanned the shelf with the tiny brown bottles of fragrances, neatly stored in alphabetical order.

Alaskan Wild Berries. Almond Vanilla. Amaretto Coffee. Apple and Orange Blossom.

On and on they went, overwhelming him with options.

"Okay, how are you doing over here?"

"Well... I have no idea how I'm going to narrow it down."

She smiled. "That's okay. I'm here to help. Who is the candle for?"

Jared faltered. "Oh, it's for my Secret Santa gift, actually."

"Okay, that's great. Tell me about them."

Jared began to describe Alexis. "Well, she's strong

and brave. She's a good friend. Kind and sweet. Kind of snarky, which I enjoy."

Ashley's smiled broadened. "She sounds lovely."

Jared sighed. "Yeah, she really is."

The shopkeeper pressed her lips together and scanned the fragrances. "Are you thinking woodsy or floral or foodie?"

Jared raised his eyebrows at the question. "Oh. Ummm, not floral. She doesn't like floral scents. Woodsy, I guess? But not masculine. She's strong... but she's still... vulnerable, you know?"

Ashley pulled a few bottles off the shelf, reaching in seemingly random patterns until she had a row of ten lined up on the shelf.

"Now, these are very concentrated, and we'll only use a bit of each one. But go through these and dismiss any that you don't like offhand." She showed him the proper way to waft the aroma toward him instead of inhaling straight from the bottle.

Jared smelled each one, setting aside four that made his nose wrinkle.

Ashley looked at the remaining scents. "Oh, this is going to be nice, I can tell. You've got a good nose. Let me just make a suggestion."

She pulled one last bottle from the shelf, set a few others away, and pulled out a small bowl. She squeezed five or so drops from one bottle, three from another, and one from the last two. She stirred the fragrances together and then invited him to take a whiff.

Jared inhaled the combination, his eyes widening at the inviting sweet and smoky concoction. "How'd you do that?" he asked in amazement.

Ashley laughed. "Well, you did most of it. But I've been doing this a long time. You start to get a feel for how things blend."

"I love it. It's perfect for her."

He watched with interest as Ashley took some melted wax and mixed in the fragrances they had chosen in a smaller pot. "You stir this," she said.

"For how long."

"Until I say to stop," she said with a wink.

He stirred and stirred and stirred for what seemed like forever. The timer went off and Ashley came back with two jars.

"We'll fill this one for your girl. And whatever is left, we'll pour in this smaller one for you to take," she explained.

"Thanks. This is perfect. I can't wait to give it to her."

"It'll be ready to pick up tomorrow. But you shouldn't light them for at least four days. Preferably longer. This gives the oils time to cure in the soy wax."

Jared nodded. "Okay, I can handle that."

Alexis's gift would be a few days later this week, but that was okay. Christmas was still two weeks from today, which gave him plenty of time to give her this candle and the last gift. And hopefully convince her that she should give him a chance as more than a friend.

ALEXIS PULLED her scarf around her face as she climbed out of Jared's truck. "I can't believe you let Tessa rope you into this," she said.

Jared waited for her a few steps ahead, and once she was next to him, they hurried across the small parking lot.

"Apparently, she promised Shayla she would participate before she got that nasty cold. She didn't want to give anything to the residents here."

Alexis shivered in the bitterly cold wind whipping under the overhang in front of the nursing home. "I'm sure glad the caroling is inside this year. I love Shayla, but there's no way I'm traipsing door-to-door. Even for her."

"I think the nursing home was a good idea. Some of these folks don't have any family to visit them. I'm sure it gets lonely."

Jared held the door open and they were greeted with a warm blast of air in the entryway.

"Ahhh, that's better," she said, unwrapping her scarf.

"Aren't Marines supposed to be tough, Alonzo?" Jared asked, bumping her shoulder with his.

She narrowed her eyes at the dig and the use of her last name. "Better watch it, Keen. I had to do my cold weather training, but I didn't have to like it."

They listened to Pastor Stephens give instructions to the group from church. There was a nice mix of children and adults. They broke into smaller groups and visited a few of the residents directly in their rooms.

Shayla knocked on the door of one room and stepped inside. Alexis could barely see the elderly woman sitting in a recliner, a blanket over her lap. Her expression was blank and disinterested.

"Hi there! We're here from Freedom Bible Church, singing some Christmas carols. Do you have a favorite we could sing for you?"

Alexis didn't hear the response, but Shayla turned to the small group huddled outside the doorway. "That's a great choice. 'Silent Night,' everyone?"

Traces of a smile danced on the woman's face as she listened to their voices. Jared's strong baritone sounded over her shoulder, and she began to harmonize with the melody. When the song ended, the woman clapped weakly.

She said something to Shayla that Alexis didn't catch.

"We hope you have a Merry Christmas, Elsie." Shayla's voice was kind and sweet as she patted Elsie gently on the hand before they moved on to the next room.

After a few more stops, they went to the recreation room and met up with the other groups. The room was filled with residents, in chairs and wheelchairs, at tables and lining the walls. A few residents laughed and smiled, watching the children in their caroling group pester their parents about the table of cookies along one wall.

Nursing staff were scattered among the residents.

Pastor Stephens said a few words to the gathered group of residents and staff, expressing the joy of the season and the gift of Jesus for every person. Then he called out songs for the group to sing. Some of the residents joined in, while others chose to watch.

She spotted a few of the men with War Veteran ball caps on, proudly proclaiming their military service, despite being indoors and nearly 8 p.m. Alexis felt a twinge of guilt about her reluctance to participate in the event.

It was a simple thing, really. But the smiles on their faces would stick with her long after they left. Jared's words came back to her mind. Some of the people here didn't have any family to visit them. Or perhaps their family lived far away.

She was blessed to have the friends she had here in Freedom. She couldn't let herself take that for granted. Full of gratitude, she wrapped her fingers around Jared's arm and enjoyed the way their voices melded together on the chorus of "Angels We Have Heard on High."

JARED PLACED his hand over top of Alexis's as it rested on his bicep. She wasn't singing loudly, but her sweet alto added depth to the array of voices. He hadn't known she could sing.

Another piece of the Alexis puzzle.

After the songs ended, the group spread out around the room. He guided Alexis toward a table of what he judged to be fairly grumpy old men. He wasn't sure exactly why, but he felt like maybe they were her kind of people. There was one empty chair and he gestured for Alexis to take it.

"Hey, fellas. Merry Christmas," he said with a smile.

One man grunted. The other two replied unenthusiastically.

"Merry Christmas."

"Don't you two have something better to do on a

Wednesday night than hang out with us old geezers?"

Alexis smiled. "I don't know about him," she pointed up at Jared, "but I actually just came for the cookies."

This made one of the men crack a smile. "I could go for a cookie, I suppose."

Jared perked up. "I'll go grab a bunch for the table, all right?"

He left Alexis there and filled a plate full of cookies for the table. When he came back, Alexis had worked some form of magic, because the three old men were laughing and smiling.

"Now, this guy? He was in the Chair Force. We just let him hang with us because we feel sorry for him."

The Air Force veteran growled. "Argh. Don't listen to him, young lady. Those Army grunts are all spit, no polish. Of course, you already know that, being a Marine."

Alexis laughed and grabbed a cookie. "When did you all serve?"

Jared watched, amazed at how Alexis connected with the old veterans. They regaled each other with stories from boot camp and asked Alexis questions about how things had changed.

The men ate their cookies and talked about their

pasts, all while Jared and Alexis asked questions to keep them talking.

"Do you ever wish it had been different? That you hadn't been drafted?" Alexis asked the group. Jared couldn't help but wonder what was driving the question. Did she regret her own experiences?

The Navy veteran who had served in Korea clicked his tongue and nodded. "Sometimes. It's hard not to wonder, anyway. There are things you wish you hadn't seen." His voice grew pensive. "Hadn't done." He cleared his throat. "But you can't go back. You just press forward. Pray more. Hold your loved ones tightly."

Alexis nodded. "That's pretty good advice," she said quietly.

The man looked up to where Jared was standing behind Alexis. "You take good care of her, all right?"

Jared swallowed thickly. He nodded. "I will."

If she'd let him, Jared knew that he'd stand by Alex until they were sitting in matching wheelchairs in the nursing home.

10

$\mathcal{B}$y Friday, Alexis was dreading the evening. When she'd tried to postpone number seven's blind date so she could go to Ty and Addison's Christmas party, Toby's brilliant solution was for her to bring her date with her.

She slipped on her "ugly sweater," that morning, which made her smile every time she thought about it. It had, of course, been a gift from Jared last year when she'd tried to skip the annual party because she didn't have one.

The large gingerbread man on the front of the sweater was missing a piece of his head, complete with teeth marks. The words Bite Me were neatly knitted in green on the red sweater. Leave it to Jared to find the perfect way to take her grumpy demeanor and turn it into a joke.

She shouldn't enjoy it so much, but she loved the way he was able to soften some of her rough edges. Why he continued to do so was the part she didn't really understand.

Her friends at the nursing home probably would have enjoyed the sweater. She'd ended up having a great time taking part in the caroling event. The group of cranky old war vets was exactly what she needed. Freedom was full of prior service members, but she didn't often talk to people about her service. It had been exactly what she needed to break the ice with those guys. Well, that and cookies.

Because she secretly enjoyed the disapproving looks she got from some of Freedom's stodgiest members, she met with Tessa for lunch wearing her gingerbread man sweater.

She watched Tessa's face as she pulled off her coat and laughed when Tessa rolled her eyes. "That sweater is awful. I can't believe you are wearing it around town."

Alexis grinned. "What? I like it. Besides, you're the one who is going to have flashing Christmas lights attached to your sweater tonight."

Tessa's eyes lit up. "Oh, not only that. This year, I made a hat that has a giant gold star on top. With my green sweater and the lights, I'm a whole tree!"

Alexis just laughed at Tessa's enthusiasm and

enjoyed the light and joy that radiated from her friend while they ate their lunch.

When they were finished, Alexis said, "I'm glad you're feeling better and we were able to do this. I know we work together and all, but sometimes I feel like I barely see you."

Tessa smiled. "I know what you mean. This time of year is crazy, and ever since the wedding, I just feel like I can't keep up with everyone."

The server brought back their credit cards and set a gift bag in front of Alexis. She looked up in confusion. "What's this?"

The server simply shrugged and walked away. Alexis gave Tessa a confused look. "Did you do this?"

"No, but open it! It's probably from your Secret Santa, right?" Tessa's excitement was obvious.

That made sense. Honestly, it had been nearly two weeks since she received the flowers, she'd almost forgotten about the gift exchange. Her gift to Trudy had been delivered on Tuesday, courtesy of the United States Postal Service.

She was not nearly as creative as her own Secret Santa, apparently. She looked around, trying to pick out who it might be in the small cafe.

"Come on, we're almost late for Heath's one o'clock meeting."

"Fine, fine. Hold your horses."

Alexis reached into the bag and found a candle

from Wick and Sarcasm. "Oh," she said. She could hear the disappointment in her own voice. Which wasn't entirely fair, since she'd gifted Trudy a candle very similar. She'd just been spoiled with the other gifts.

Without looking at the label, she pulled off the lid and smelled the gift. The warm aroma of wood and vanilla greeted her. It was different. Unique. She liked it. Turning the jar around, she sought out the name.

The label was her favorite shade of orange, a dark, earthy color. But the words on the label caused her breath to catch.

Alexis.

"What is it?" Tessa asked.

She turned the candle around and slid it across the table.

Hurriedly, she dug through the gift bag to find the card, desperate to see what the message was.

Dear Alexis,

In you, I see the perfect blend of strength and vulnerability. This "Alexis" candle has cedarwood for your strength like the towering cedars of the woods on the mountain, smoke for your resilience after the refining fire *of trials, hints of vanilla and sugar for your sweet spirit, and a touch of cinnamon for your spicy wit.*

WITHOUT JUST ONE OF THESE, *the candle would not be complete, just like you are the sum of your parts. Each part of you is treasured beyond compare by those who see you.*

COMPLETELY YOURS,
   Your Secret Santa

HUNGRY FOR THE message of approval and adoration, she reread the message again. And again. Until Tessa pulled the card from her hands.

Her friend sighed. "Oohhh, that's so flipping sweet. Who is this person and why are you not married to him?"

Alexis made a face at her. "Come on. It's just someone being nice. I don't know, maybe it's Heath?" She couldn't figure out who knew her well enough to write a note like that. "Besides, the hand-writing definitely looks like a girl."

It was Tessa's turn to make a face. "Yeah, you're right. I love my brother, but there is no way he's coming up with something like that. Besides, Claire couldn't convince him to do the Secret Santa anyway. I already asked."

Alexis frowned, then grabbed the card back from Tessa's hands. "Doesn't matter anyway. It's just a candle." She stood up and began the walk through the restaurant toward the door.

"Just a candle? Are you kidding me right now?" Tessa chased after her, voicing her objections while Alexis made her way out.

The entire ride back to Got Your Six, Tessa went on and on about how amazing the candle was and how the person giving the gifts must be someone special, and she needed to find out who it was.

Alexis sat mostly silent, letting her friend's chattering fade into the background as she considered the words of her Secret Santa. They claimed that people who saw all of her, loved all of her.

But it wasn't true. Because no one saw all of her, other than the Lord.

Which she kept telling herself was enough.

She didn't need to let anyone else in. Once these blind dates were over, she could retreat back into her little existence with work and church and occasional fun with friends like Tessa and Jared.

They might love the parts of her they'd seen.

But they hadn't seen it all.

∾

THAT NIGHT, Chase was picking her up from Got Your Six, because she wasn't about to tell a stranger her home address. He was a friend of Toby's, apparently visiting from out of town. Though why Toby was passing him off on her was a mystery.

He was waiting by his car when she came out. The evening was dark and chilly, and she tugged her hat down around her ears as she crossed the parking lot.

Chase spoke as she got closer. "You must be Alexis." He let out a wolf whistle. "Dang, Toby didn't say you were so hot!"

Her eyebrows skyrocketed. "Excuse me?"

"What? It's a compliment, babe."

Alexis couldn't believe her ears. What was Toby thinking, setting her up with this overgrown buffoon?

She let the icy disapproval fill her voice. "Don't ever call me 'babe' again, got it?"

"Chill out. I'm just saying you're hot. And I like your sweater."

She actually wished she could get away with wearing it more than one night of the year, but it was probably a bit too rude to wear anywhere but a party like this one. And maybe it would keep Chase from getting any ideas.

Although judging by the completely inappropriate actions of the deer on his Christmas sweater, he wasn't exactly concerned about crossing any boundaries.

She was desperately tempted to just put this guy in his place and cancel the whole thing. But he was a friend of Toby's, which was the only reason she hadn't left after the first comment. There was no way she was getting in his car.

"So, I actually need to bring my car to the party as well. Why don't you just follow me in yours?"

"Oh? I can just ride with you," he said, standing up straight.

"No," she said firmly. "I would feel more comfortable driving separately."

Chase held his hands up. "No problem, ba–I mean, Alexis."

At least, maybe he was trainable.

"I'll see you there," she said tightly.

The entire way to the party, she prayed for the rest of the evening. She could tell Chase was trouble. But she didn't want to hurt Toby.

When she arrived at Ty and Addison's place, cars already lined the street and she had to park several houses away. Chase pulled in directly behind her. She took a deep breath before pushing the car door open and forcing a smile.

"You drive like my grandma, babe."

So much for new tricks.

She rolled her eyes and headed toward the house.

"Come on, don't be like that, babe," he called after her.

She whirled around, her heart racing as she prepared to dress him down. He was completely clueless. She was more than capable of taking care of herself. But as he took a lumbering step toward her in the snow, her body reacted. Deep in her mind, Alexis knew that she didn't need to be scared of him. But her body wasn't listening. Everything within her tensed up. Her vision narrowed, focused only on the perceived threat in front of her.

Her heart thumped loudly in her ears and she felt strangely detached from her limbs as she raised her arms and stumbled backward, trying to get away.

"What the heck?" Chase's confusion barely registered. Her chest was tight and she gasped for breath. It didn't make sense. Even as it was happening, she knew there was nothing to be afraid of. But her body didn't seem to get the memo.

She held up her hand to stop Chase from coming closer.

Desperate to get ahold of herself, she forced herself to take deeper breaths than felt possible. She lowered to the ground, barely feeling the cold seeping through her jeans.

"What's going on here?"

Jared's voice cracked through the isolating tunnel of panic.

He was running toward them, yelling questions.

She shook her head, unable to respond with her lack of air. The pieces began to settle, though, Jared's presence at least partially calming her agitated state, despite his own yelling.

"Who are you? What did you do to her?"

11

---

*J*ared tore his eyes from Alexis's position on the ground and glared at the bulky blond guy a few steps away from her.

His blood was running hot, despite the bitter evening air. He hadn't seen them until he'd heard Alexis yell, then he'd seen her stumble backward and sit down. Zeroing in on her, he'd barely noticed the man walking toward her, but when she'd held a hand up to stop him, Jared had felt himself go rigid.

A hundred scenarios had played instantly in his mind, some too terrible to entertain. But other than her heavy breathing and concerning position on the ground, Alexis looked unharmed.

"I didn't do anything, man. We were just headed to the party."

Jared took one look at Alexis, who was finally

looking at them instead of the ground between her knees. In her wide eyes, he saw the panic and horror. She looked away again. "I don't think so, buddy."

"Aww, come on. She's fine," the insensitive jerk insisted.

"Hey, y'all. What's going on?"

Jared turned to see Toby approaching them from the other side of the street. When Toby noticed Alexis, his expression grew troubled. "Chase, what happened to Alexis?"

"I don't know. We were just headed inside and the crazy lady flipped out on me."

Jared stepped toward the man. "She's not crazy," he said emphatically. "And if Alex got upset with you, I know without a doubt there was a good reason for it."

"Look, Toby. Your girl is hot, I'm not going to deny that, but I don't have time for a crazy chick. Let's bounce."

Toby reared back. "What? Dude, do you even hear yourself? I don't know what prompted this little visit of yours, but you are not the guy I knew ten years ago. I think it's time for you to leave."

Chase lifted his chin and clicked his tongue. "Pssh. Whatever, man. This town is lame, anyway. Can't believe you left The Big Easy for this little mountain map dot."

"Let's go. I want you to get your stuff out of my place and hit the road. Tonight."

With Toby handling his so-called friend, Jared slowly crossed the snow and crouched in front of Alexis. "Hey, sweetheart. Are you okay?" She nodded, but he could hear the rapid, shallow breathing continue. He kept his voice gentle, unsure what else to do. He'd never seen her like this.

"Can you look at me, Alex. I just need to see you." She lifted her head, exhaling slowly through her mouth. "That's my girl," he said proudly.

She repeated the breath, her eyes falling closed. A tear fell from one, drying quickly as it left a trail down her cheek. His heart caught in his throat, desperate to make her pain stop. He was walking on eggshells, not sure what the right move would be.

He wanted to pull her into his arms, but he felt like it would be the wrong move.

Instead, he lowered himself to the snow next to her and gently laid his hand on her back, rubbing slowly. She shuddered, her shoulders sagging and her back pressing into the contact. "It's okay. I'm here. Everything's okay." He continued murmuring the reassurances as she inhaled and exhaled deliberately. He didn't know much about it, but he suspected this was a panic attack, and from what he knew, Alexis was handling it like a pro.

A few minutes later, she whispered, "I'm okay, Jared. You should go."

Typical Alexis.

"I don't think so, sweetheart." He extended his arm across her back and pulled her gently into his side. "Pretty sure you're stuck with me tonight."

His butt was getting cold though, and he had to imagine hers was too.

"Come on, I'll take you home. And you can either tell me all about it or we can turn on Faithmark movies and make popcorn."

The edge of her lips lifted, though she didn't outright agree. He stood, then extended a hand to help her to her feet, grateful when she took it.

He walked her to his truck and helped her inside. A shiver made her teeth rattle, so he cranked the heat and grabbed a blanket from the backseat for her. He still didn't know what had happened, but the urge to find Chase and deck him for whatever he'd done to cause this was growing stronger.

He drove in silence, knowing Alexis wouldn't appreciate being pushed. It didn't mean the desire to ask all his questions was dissipating. The truth was that Alexis would tell him only what she wanted to tell him—when she wanted to tell him.

After four years, he knew that much was true.

Which meant he would spend this short drive praying that she would finally open up.

12
———

*A*lexis stared straight ahead as Jared drove, her panic attack subsiding but leaving her with a barrage of humiliation and wounded pride. She hadn't had a panic attack in almost a year. And never in front of anyone. Let alone in front of Jared.

If there was anyone in Freedom that she wished she could hide her diagnosis from, it was Jared, who sometimes looked at her like she was the most perfect creation in all the world. Surely, that would stop now. When he realized what a messed up psyche she really carried around.

What could she tell him tonight that wouldn't make her sound insane? Chase had said he didn't have time for the crazy chick. Which was basically the same message that her mom had given her four years ago in California.

Putting up with Alexis's problems was too much effort. She had too much damage.

And it wasn't as if she wanted Chase to stay. But she desperately wanted Jared to. The idea that he might decide not to stick around after seeing this had the tears welling up behind her eyes and nose.

She sniffed, trying to pull herself together.

Jared turned his head toward her at the sound and she looked toward the window. She wasn't ready to face him.

It was only a couple of minutes before they pulled into her driveway. "What about my car?" The question came out more forcefully than she intended, but the thought hadn't even occurred to her when they left Ty and Addison's street.

"I'll get it taken care of. Don't worry about a thing, okay?"

Alexis nodded. It wasn't in her nature not to worry or think through every detail. But it was admittedly kind of nice to know that she trusted that if Jared said he would take care of it, he would. "Okay. Thanks, by the way," she added in a gentler tone.

"No thanks necessary. Let's just get you inside."

"I'm fine, really. You should go back to the party."

Her words were at complete odds with her heart, which was practically jumping up and down throwing a tantrum at her for telling him to leave.

"I'm staying," he replied firmly. "I'll leave later tonight. But I can call Tessa if you'd rather have her here all night with you?"

Alexis softened further at his thoughtful suggestion. But she didn't want Tessa, as much as she loved her friend. "No, that's okay. I'd rather have you, I think."

Jared's wide smile was her reward for that admission. Any regret she might have had for the uncharacteristic vulnerability vanished with his tender expression.

Once they got inside, Jared settled her onto the couch with a blanket before disappearing into the kitchen. A few moments later, he came back with a mug of peppermint hot chocolate. He'd removed his hat and boots. His jacket was gone too, revealing his ugly Christmas sweater.

She grabbed the hot cocoa from his hands as she read the message on the shirt out loud. "Kiss me under the mistletoe…"

Jared looked around the room, an innocent expression on his face. "Oh, well. If you insist. I'm sure there's some mistletoe around here somewhere… Let me just—"

She laughed. "What would you do if someone really found some mistletoe?"

"Oh, I wasn't planning on waiting. I brought my own." He rifled through his jacket pocket on the armrest behind him and pulled out a sprig of mistletoe. "See?" He held it over his head. "It's an open invitation, really."

His dark-brown eyes slid to hers, the puppy dog impression back in full force.

"I see," she said.

Slowly, she put her hot chocolate on the coffee table next to the Alexis candle and scooted slightly toward him. He didn't move a muscle as she leaned closer, glancing up at the fake mistletoe he held above them.

She crossed the distance between them, unsure of what her own plan was, even as she felt the overwhelming temptation to press her lips to his.

"Alexis," he whispered, his voice full of warning.

His eyes moved to her lips, and her heart stopped. She altered course and skimmed her lips against his cheek, pressing her eyes closed against the disappointment and drinking in the feel of his stubble on her skin. His spicy cologne filled her lungs, not quite erasing the pleasantly familiar scent of the dogs he spent so much time with.

As much as she wanted that kiss, it would be a mistake. This evening had been case in point about why she couldn't push things with Jared.

He deserved someone who could go to a party without having a panic attack in the snow outside. A little voice niggled in her mind that perhaps she wouldn't have had the panic attack if she'd been with Jared instead of Chase.

But that wasn't enough.

She pulled back, pasting a smile on her face. Jared's expression was clouded.

"Pretty convenient," she joked, as though her entire world hadn't just come crashing to a head. "I'm sure you would have been quite popular with the single ladies at the party."

Jared cleared his throat and tossed the mistletoe on the table. "Yeah, well. If last year is any indication, the only single woman who was going to be there was you."

Alexis tried to ignore the implication of that remark and turn their conversation back to the teasing banter she loved so much. "You never know. Maybe a tourist or two scored an invite."

He shot her a pained expression. "Alexis," he started.

She held her breath, afraid to hear what he was going to say. Afraid she wouldn't be able to resist what he would offer.

But Jared seemed to reconsider his own words as well. He shook his head and then started over. "So what will it be? Are you going to tell me what happened tonight? Or are we watching *Christmas with the Firefighter* for the third year in a row?"

"Hey. I happen to like *Christmas with the Fire-*

fighter. That Krystal Daughtry is the best actress on Faithmark these days."

Jared shrugged. "If you say so. I think you've just got a thing for the firefighter. Maybe I should call Connor and see if he can stay the evening with you." Jared's joking tone let her know there was no malice in the seemingly jealous words.

"You know there's no one else I'd rather be with tonight than you." She wanted to reassure him. He needed to know how much she appreciated him and his friendship.

He gave a small smile. "Yeah. I know."

"So popcorn then?" She forced a smile. Jared might have seen her breakdown slightly tonight, but it wasn't that bad. Everything would be totally fine. They'd watch a movie, hang out, and he would go home. Tomorrow, she could pretend he'd never seen her hyperventilating in the snow.

If she didn't acknowledge it, then Jared would be none the wiser. He wouldn't know that she was broken.

If he didn't know about her condition, he wouldn't decide that he didn't have time for the "crazy chick" either. It was the only way to keep things the way they were now. And while it might not include real kisses under the mistletoe, this friendship was going to have to suffice.

JARED LEFT Alexis's house shortly after the movie and the disappointing result to the evening. The good-bye was as awkward an exchange as they'd ever had. But he was focusing on the good. Even though Alexis hadn't opened up, he felt like they'd crossed a bridge of sorts. The episode at the party was scary for him; he couldn't imagine what it had been like for her.

But she'd let him stay for a few hours. And she seemed mostly fine when he left. The way she'd leaned in and kissed his cheek under the mistletoe? He didn't think his heart would ever recover from the absolute carnival ride she'd taken him on.

He'd wanted to ask why... but the timing wasn't right. It had been a long evening. And when he was ready to have that conversation with Alexis, he knew it needed to be the right time. God's time.

The weekend crawled by, leading into the last full week before Christmas. The Christmas parade was coming up on Friday, and he didn't have too much time to arrange Alexis's last Secret Santa gift. He'd been considering a handmade ornament from the glassblowing shop in town, or a painting from Art and Soul. But after the events of the other night, Jared had something else in mind.

It meant paying for rush shipping, but it would be worth it.

As far as he could tell, she still didn't suspect that he was her Secret Santa. And he'd seen the candle on her coffee table, so at least she hadn't thrown it away or anything.

On Monday morning, Jared stopped by Derek's office and sat across from his long-time friend and employer.

"How's it going with Ruby for the peanut detection skills?" Derek asked.

"It's great. I think Ruby will be ready for them in January."

"Cool. What about the seizure dog? Did they ever come up with the down payment?"

"Actually, that was what I wanted to talk with you about." Jared shifted in the chair and cleared his throat. "I've been thinking about our business, and I totally understand why we have to charge so much for the dogs we graduate. There is a lot of cost involved. and then attrition... But I was thinking, if we're going to branch into more of these medical service dogs, maybe we should consider adding a non-profit arm of the company."

Derek pursed his lips in thought. "What does that mean? What's the advantage?"

Jared continued. "Well, I was talking to Kyle–the father buying Ruby for his daughter? He was interested in donating to cover the cost for other families who weren't able to get a dog like he was. So I've been looking into it. If we have a separate non-profit, people could donate to cover expenses for training certain dogs. People could apply for the grants. Like Laura and Parker, who need the seizure dog."

Derek gave a hum of interest. "I think it sounds really intriguing. You know my background. Working in the military, I just assumed those dogs were where DK9 would find its niche. But you've brought us a ton of other opportunities in other arenas. I think it's a great idea, and if you think you want to take it on, I'll support you in any way I can. I think Megan and I would consider making the first donation to the newly formed organization."

Jared grinned, unable to hide his relief and excitement at the encouragement of his mentor. "Really? Thanks, D. That means a lot. I'd say we make it our goal for next year to get everything in line and hold our first fundraiser. What do you say?"

"Let's do it."

They finished catching up about the schedule for the week and any upcoming projects, before Jared went back to his office. He pulled out his phone and texted Alexis.

Jared: Derek is on board with a non-profit arm of DK9!

Jared: Also, good morning. Can we have lunch?

Alexis: Congrats!

Alexis: I'd like that. El Cresta at 11:30?

He sent back a thumbs up. When it was time for lunch, he got a table and waited for Alexis. He expected it to be awkward, but when she came to the table, it was as if nothing had changed. She looked a bit frazzled when she sat down.

"So, am I supposed to ration your chips and salsa today?"

She grunted at him. "Don't even think about it. It has been the most Monday-esque Monday that ever was. I need carbohydrate therapy."

He chuckled and slid the basket toward her side of the table.

"Want to tell Doctor Jared all about it?"

She rolled her eyes and munched on a chip. "Toby keeps checking on me and apologizing for Chase's behavior Friday night. I'm glad he realized that his friend was a jerk, but I'm just ready to move on, you know?"

A half dozen times during the movie, he'd been tempted to press her about what had happened with Chase. Had he tried to make a move on her? Intimidate her?

Jared hated that he didn't have any answers. Toby swore up and down that Chase hadn't done anything to set Alexis off. Which created more questions than it answered.

Jared nodded, but he knew Toby felt guilty. He'd texted Jared a few more times over the weekend to see how Alexis was doing. "He just wants to make sure you're okay."

"I'm fine! Why does everyone keep asking me that? It was no big deal. I'm totally fine."

Jared raised his eyebrows at her outburst, which made her groan and lay her forehead down on the table.

"Ugh. Even you don't believe me, do you?" her voice was muffled, since she spoke directly toward the floor.

"We are all just trying to figure out what happened, Alex. It was a little freaky to see you all discombobulated."

She lifted her head and raised an eyebrow. "Dis-combobulated? Really?"

He shrugged. "I don't know! Yeah, discombobulated. You were on the ground, hyperventilating. Not exactly the Alexis we're all used to seeing. So, yeah. We just want to make sure you're okay."

"I'm fine," she said through gritted teeth. "Now, can we just have lunch without you trying to diagnose me?"

Jared watched for a moment, trying to read the truth in her eyes. There was something she wasn't telling him, but he didn't know what it was. Or why she was so stubbornly keeping it hidden.

He wasn't a fool. He knew that even after four years, Alexis hadn't let him in entirely. There were still pieces she kept hidden.

But he wasn't going to push her.

Oh, how he wanted to, though. He wanted to shake her by the shoulders and tell her how much he loved her and convince her she was being completely ridiculous. But he wouldn't.

Because the only thing worse than being rejected outright would be ruining their chance because of his own impatience and pushiness.

Melody had gone on and on about how she felt smothered and pushed into commitment by him. She said she felt like her only option was to leave.

So instead of declaring his feelings and trying to force Alexis to open up when she clearly didn't want to, he glanced at the menu. "I think I'm having arroz con pollo. What about you?"

13

*A*lexis returned to the office after lunch, chased by guilt about snapping at Jared. Lunch had been strained, and it was all her fault. He deserved to know the truth about her. But something was holding her back.

As much as she wanted the words in her Secret Santa gift to be true—that she was treasured by those who saw her—it just hadn't been the case in the past. When she separated from the Marines and returned home, she'd assumed her mother would be supportive and accepting. But when push came to shove, Alexis's panic attacks and dark moods were too much.

What did it say when the person who was supposed to be your lifelong support system decided you were too much trouble?

"I think it would be better if you built a new life somewhere else, sweetheart. I can't keep leaving work because you're scared of the mailman." Her mom's words, though delivered with gentle tones, had sliced her open and laid bare every insecurity Alexis had. How could she expect anyone to sign up for a life with her? Her own mother couldn't even handle it.

As much as she wanted to tell Jared the truth, she wouldn't be able to handle it if he decided she wasn't worth the effort. Better to have him as a friend and keep her secrets than to chase him off entirely. And stepping into anything more than friendship wasn't an option. It was hard enough to hide the truth when she saw him two or three times a week.

Her Secret Santa just didn't know the whole story.

At Got Your Six, Tessa found her in her office. "Hey, Alexis. What happened to you at the party? I thought you were all excited to show everyone your ridiculous sweater?"

Alexis bit back a groan. The last thing she wanted to do was admit that she'd had a panic attack and had to bail on the entire party. "Uhh, long story. But the date was a bust and I ended up hanging out at home with Jared watching a movie."

Tessa's eyebrows shot up, and Alexis felt the heat rise in her cheeks.

"Nothing like that." Except, she realized, it kind of had been exactly like that. When she'd nearly thrown herself at him under the mistletoe.

Tessa pouted. "Well, that is thoroughly disappointing. Cuddling on the couch?" she asked hopefully?

Alexis laughed. "No cuddling! I kissed him on the cheek."

Tessa gasped. "I need more details."

"That's all there was. He had mistletoe he was going to use at the party, so I kissed him." She shrugged. "Nothing to get all excited about."

She could tell by the look on Tessa's face that she wasn't buying it. "Mm-hmm. You just keep telling yourself that, lady. Jared is the perfect man for you. And it's about time you realized it."

Alexis ignored the comment. Between the Christmas caroling event and the tension on her couch under the mistletoe, she was beginning to wonder if Tessa wasn't right. As tempting as it was to entertain thoughts about a future between her and Jared, it wasn't a possibility. "Did you need something?"

Tessa looked disappointed but moved on from the topic. "Do you have plans for the Christmas parade?"

Alexis shook her head, but Toby's voice interrupted as he yelled from down the hall. "She has a date!"

Alexis groaned and laid her forehead on the desk, lifting it up and down to gently bang it on the cool, solid surface.

Tessa was unsympathetic. "Oooh, who is the date this time?"

Alexis looked up to see Toby join her friend in the doorway.

"Trevor. He works at the Lodge."

"Isn't he a bellboy?" Alexis asked, trying to match the name with a face.

"I believe the proper term is guest services attendant," Toby said with a false snooty accent, which made her smile despite her annoyance at him.

"You cannot set me up with a bellboy," she pleaded.

"Ah, ah, ah. Guest services attendant," Tessa corrected with a finger pointed upward.

Alexis rolled her eyes. "Please, Toby? After the last one, don't you think we could just not?"

Toby appeared thoughtful for a moment. "I'll tell you what. I already told Trevor about it. But if you go on this date, I'll give you double credit."

Alexis did the math. If she went to the parade with Trevor, it would count as dates eight and nine. And then she'd just have one more to be done with this whole nightmare scenario. She was never going to make a bet again.

"Fine. But after this, no dates until after New Year's."

"New Year's Eve," Toby countered quickly.

The idea of starting fresh in January with no dates on the calendar was appealing. And she could easily end a New Year's Eve date before 10 p.m. when the ball dropped at midnight in New York. She'd have nearly two weeks after the parade with no dates whatsoever.

"Deal."

Toby grinned. "You're going to love Trevor. He's a good guy."

Tessa laughed. "Isn't he like twenty-three years old?"

"He's twenty-five!"

Alexis shooed them both out of her office. Her date with Trevor was Friday Alexis's problem. Until then, she'd be working on the details for Chris Tooley's consulting firm. And counting down the days until her Secret Santa left her last gift. Even if she didn't agree with their kind words, they were nice to receive. She still had no idea who this person was, and she was hoping they would reveal themselves with the last gift.

~

Jared stroked Maverick's fur. "I'm sorry, buddy. You're a really good dog, and someone is going to love you so much."

Maverick stared back up at him with big brown eyes, full of trust and affection. This was the hardest part of the job. He always dragged his feet when it came time to dismiss dogs from the program. But it had to be done.

Maverick had just failed his final test and was officially out of the running to be a SAR dog.

Jared couldn't shake the idea that he'd be a great dog for Alexis. But with the way they'd left things after the incident at the party, he didn't want to push her.

Instead, he set the adoption paperwork to the side of his desk. He could drag his feet a bit longer on finding Maverick an adoptive home. He wasn't a fan of Christmas gift adoptions anyway. Too many of them ended up being rehomed a year or two later after the parents decided a dog was too much work for little Joey.

"You can just come home with me for a week or two, right, Mav? Chewy will love the company."

He walked Maverick back to the kennel and then finished up the notes on Maverick's file. He made sure to note that failure wasn't behavior or obedience related, but simply that Maverick's nose wasn't quite skilled enough for the job. A knock on the door of his office interrupted him a while later. Derek stood in the doorway.

"You headed out?"

Derek nodded. "Alabama, here we come. Oh, and this came for you." Derek set a white box on his desk.

"I hope you have a great trip," Jared said, reaching for the package.

"Thanks. I think it'll be good. Megan's looking forward to seeing her folks."

"And not seeing the snow, I'm sure."

His boss laughed. "Yeah, there is that too. She turned in her next book to the publisher, so she's officially in vacation mode."

Jared shook his head. "I don't know how she comes up with all those ideas. So cool."

It was a well-kept secret in the world–and a poorly kept secret in Freedom–that Megan was actually Marcus Warner, the acclaimed author of adventure thrillers. Her latest release was on the New York Times Bestseller list and was likely to be wrapped up under many Christmas trees this year.

"Ooh, more cookies." Jared wasn't going to complain about his Secret Santa at all. He offered one to Derek. "Do you need anything from me while you're gone?"

Derek shook his head while he grabbed a snick-erdoodle. "Nah. I'm leaving Libby and Dobby here.

You and Amber have the schedule worked out for taking care of everybody, right?"

Jared nodded. "Yep. We'll keep the chaos mostly under control."

There were anywhere between six and eight dogs in various stages of training at DK9 at any given time. Add in Derek's two dogs and Chewy, who came to work with Jared most days, and the kennel was never quiet.

"See you next year!" Jared quipped as Derek turned to leave.

He couldn't help but wonder if next year would be any different from this one. He had one more gift to give Alexis. If it didn't make her see him in a new light, then it seemed like he'd be destined to stay in the friendzone forever.

JARED CAREFULLY UNWRAPPED THE PACKAGE, pulling out the special antique he'd found on eBay. It was perfect for Alexis. And maybe it, along with the note he planned, would be enough to convince her that she should trust him. This note he penned in his own handwriting, praying over each word.

He wanted to see her open it.

If he delivered it at the parade somehow, he might be able to observe without being too suspicious. Toby had already told him that Alexis had another blind date during the parade. He was so ready for these dates to be over. He wasn't sure which was worse, the good ones like Connor, or the bad ones like Chase.

He'd tried to convince Toby to drop the whole thing, but the New Orleans native had been adamant about the terms of the bet being fulfilled. But there had been a twinkle in his eye when he agreed to help Jared out. Maybe that explained all the bad dates.

The afternoon of the parade, Jared grabbed the small package and the envelope, tucking it into his coat pocket. He found the start of the parade and scanned the waiting cars and floats.

When his eyes landed on Pete's insurance company float, he flagged down Jan, who was waiting alongside the car, which was decked out in garland and lights.

"Good morning!"

"Hey, Jan. Are you sure you are still up for being my delivery man?"

Jan grinned. "Oh yes, definitely. Anything I can do to help."

Jared smiled back. "Well, thank you." He pulled the small package from his coat pocket and handed it to her. "Alexis likes to watch the parade from the corner by Evelyn's. I can't guarantee that's where she'll be though."

Jan tucked the box into the back seat of the convertible, among the bags of candy they'd be throwing to the crowd. "Don't you worry. I'll find her! It's about time you two got together," she said, leaning in with a conspiratorial smile.

Jared shrugged. "Well, I have to admit, I think so too. I just don't know if Alexis agrees."

Jan patted him on the shoulder. "It'll all work out how it is supposed to, young man."

"Thanks, Jan. Have a great parade." He turned in a circle, arms spread, as he backed away. "It's a beautiful day!"

"Sure beats a blizzard," Jan replied, chuckling. After the parade had been canceled years ago due to a huge snowstorm, everyone in town joked that any other weather was a good day for a Christmas parade. Today actually was. The sun was just beginning to dip below the buildings and the air was cool but still.

Jared hurried over toward Evelyn's, trying to spot Alexis without being seen himself.

A few moments later, he saw her and her date, who appeared not much older than a high schooler, sitting on the sidewalk in collapsible bag chairs. He found a tree in the grass in front of Evelyn's and tucked himself behind it, out of her sightline.

ALEXIS WATCHED the children in front of them eagerly looking down the street for the first signs of the parade. They clutched plastic grocery bags between gloved hands and harassed their parents with "how much longer" questions.

"How long have you worked at the resort, Trevor?" she asked.

"Almost six years," he replied proudly. "I'm just seasonal help, actually. It's a pretty sweet life, though. I spend my summers surfing in California and my winters skiing here." That explained the southern California surfer accent she was hearing. It brought flashbacks from high school.

"Oh, I didn't realize that."

Trevor grinned, his shaggy blond hair falling into his eyes. He swung his neck to flip it back to his forehead. "Yep. The tips are good, and I get a free lift pass each year. I know some of the other season chasers move around to different resorts all the time, but I kinda like coming back to Freedom each year."

Another hair flip.

She smiled. "Yeah. There's something special about this place, isn't there?"

They watched as the parade came down the street, led by the local high school marching band. Alexis had fun waving to her friends who were taking part in the parade, and watched with some anxiety as children scrambled in the street for the candy being thrown.

She waved to Jan. The older woman's face brightened and she held up a finger, rushing to get something from the back of the convertible. Alexis squinted, trying to see what Jan was holding as she came toward her. Jan squeezed through the throng of children and held out a small box.

Alexis straightened in her chair. "What's this?"

Jan grinned. "Just a special delivery from your Secret Santa!"

Alexis's eyes widened. "It was you? That makes so much sense." She laughed. That explained why the person knew her so well and was so kind in the notes. She had never suspected Jan.

Jan shook her head. "Oh no, it's not me! I'm just an elf today. But open it!" she yelled before she rushed to catch up with the O'Roarke Insurance Agency float.

Alexis frowned in confusion. If it wasn't Jan, who could it be?

She slipped her finger under the edge of the flap on the envelope, ripping it open and pulling out the familiar Christmas-style notecard.

As she read the card, the sound of the parade disappeared. The handwriting was different. Masculine.

. . .

Dear Alexis,

Whenever you feel lost, I hope you know where to find your true North. You can always count on the Lord to guide you through darkness.

And there are others who will always be there beside you. Nothing will be too much, if we go together, with the Lord in front of us.

Forever yours,
   Your Secret Santa

Tears welled up in her eyes, letting the message sink in. Curious what the gift might be, she slipped the lid off the pretty colored box. Nestled in soft layers of fabric was the most beautiful brass marine compass she'd ever seen.

She traced the metal instrument with her finger, admiring the craftsmanship of the small engraved numbers. There was a slip of paper in the box and she skimmed it. The sextant was a replica of the 1753 J Scott London Sextant, used by sailors for decades.

Very few people knew of her love of marine military history. In fact, she was pretty sure there was only one in Freedom who did.

She looked around, trying to find him in the crowd.

"Whoa, that's sweet!" Trevor's excited voice was accompanied by a hand reaching for the small box in her lap. He grabbed onto the corner of the box, and Alexis pulled it away, not wanting to share the special gift. It was fragile and probably quite expensive. She watched in horror as the gift slipped off her lap and fell to the ground with a quiet crash.

"Oh, man. I'm so sorry."

Alexis pressed her lips together, determined not to cry. She reached for the box and tried moving different parts of the instrument. She groaned in disappointment. The glass in the horizon viewer was broken, as was the mirror.

She was warm everywhere, as the horror and embarrassment of the situation washed over her. Jared had gotten her the most thoughtful gift. Four incredibly thoughtful gifts, actually. And this one was broken due to her own carelessness.

Tears spilled over her lashes and she stared down at the broken sextant. Underneath the box, the card with the sweet note mocked her. True north, eh?

Jared was delusional. What was it he'd said? Nothing was too much?

He couldn't possibly say that. She would ruin everything, just like she'd broken his beautiful gift.

Then those familiar dark eyes were in front of her as he kneeled on the sidewalk, looking up. A blue stocking hat was pulled down over his ears. "Hey, don't cry," Jared whispered.

"It's ruined," she said through tears and sniffs.

He shook his head with a soft smile. "It's fine, Alex. Just a trinket. It's nothing."

She hung her head again. "It wasn't nothing. It was perfect. The perfect gift. You know me so well."

That made him chuckle. "Yeah, well. I've sort of made it my mission to know you completely. I'd say I was doing a pretty good job of it, right?"

She smiled and nodded, but continued to stare at the broken gift. "Yeah."

Jared's tone grew serious. "I mean what I wrote, Alexis. There's nothing I wouldn't walk through to be with you. Nothing we can't handle together."

Alexis glanced up, meeting his eyes with her own. He was so handsome, and the way he locked his eyes on hers had her heart racing. She'd be a fool to push him away. Everything she wanted was right there; all she had to do was agree to let Jared take care of her. Until something happened and he realized... She started to shake her head. "I can't–"

"Don't say no," he interrupted. "You don't have to

say no. You can say yes, Alexis. And we can be together." His voice was pleading.

Slowly, as though she was emerging from under-water, the rest of the world began to creep into their conversation. The cacophony of the Christmas music blaring from a parade float, kids screaming as candy hit the street in front of them. Surfer-dude Trevor staring with wide-eyed curiosity.

Everyone was staring.

She glanced around, overwhelmed by everything going on. Intensely aware of thousands of sets of eyes on them.

"Why can't you see how good we would be together?" Jared's words were probably quiet. But in that moment, she was sure everyone was listening. Agreeing with him. Wondering why she was so broken.

Her heart rate ticked up, and heat rose in her chest as it tightened. It took every effort to force herself to take a breath against the crushing squeeze of the anxiety pressing against her. Jared was on his knees in front of her, and she was hurting him by saying no. The pressure increased.

She didn't want to hurt Jared. Saying no would hurt him now. But saying yes? Her chest squeezed tighter.

"Ho-Ho-Ho!"

She jerked at the sound of Santa over the loudspeaker. The children yelled in excitement. Breathe in. Breathe out. Slow it down. But she couldn't catch her breath.

"Don't shut me out, Alexis. I just want to talk about this. Can't you see that I love you?"

14

_J_ared watched in horror as Alexis jerked up to standing from her chair. The gift he'd so carefully selected fell to the ground, but she didn't seem to notice as she scrambled away from him.

"Alex? Where are you going?"

He followed her, ignoring the curious looks of the other parade-watchers. What was wrong with her, leaving him like that after what he said?

Oh geez. Why had he said that? It was way too much. Even if it was true, he shouldn't have blurted it out. He was supposed to have learned his lesson about coming on too strong!

But he was so tired of tiptoeing around Alexis. This was supposed to be it–his chance to convince her that they could be together. And despite her comments about how well he knew her and how perfect the gifts were... she ran away.

He slowed to a walk, trying to find Alexis on this stretch of Oak Street, away from the crowd. The sound of the parade faded as he walked. A few blocks down, he found Alexis tucked away from the street, between two houses. It was so similar to the night of the ugly sweater party, his heart broke for her.

Alexis was sucking in breaths between sobs and shudders, her head between her knees and her hands in fists by her ears.

Jared approached slowly, speaking softly. "It's okay, sweetheart. I'm here."

Alexis shook her head wildly. "No! Go away!"

He kept his voice calm as his previous frustration and hurt melted away. "I'm not going to do that, Alex. You know that. I'm staying right here."

Alexis gasped for air between words. "Fine. Then I'll leave." She started to stand but stumbled back to the ground.

He shushed her. "Don't run away. I'm just here as your friend, okay. No pressure."

She stayed silent, and he rubbed her back, letting her breathing slow and her sobs subside. Jared watched as parade-goers traipsed by, carting chairs and full bags of candy. Their joyful conversations seemed so out of place next to Alexis's obvious despair.

A twinge of guilt flared up. Was he to blame for this episode? He hadn't let it go when she'd said no. If he'd just backed off, maybe she would be there, sitting with Trevor and getting a post-parade coffee at Stories and Scones. Instead, she was sitting in the snow in a stranger's yard.

He shouldn't have pushed her. It was obvious she only wanted to be friends. If the idea of trying to be more than friends had her in a full-blown meltdown.

He tipped his head back, staring up at the sky. He'd been so sure that the Lord had arranged this opportunity for him to woo Alexis. What other explanation was there? But here he was again, driving the woman he loved away with the force of his feelings. And this time, probably losing his best friend in the process.

After several more minutes, Alexis lifted her head and sucked in a big breath of air. She blew it out slowly. Jared continued to rub his hand gently over her back.

"Are you okay?"

Alexis nodded slowly. "Yeah. I think so."

"Do you want me to drive you home?"

Alexis hesitated, and he felt the wedge between them grow even wider.

"That would be good. Thanks."

His truck was parked not too far from town square, and the crowd from the parade had mostly dispersed. He helped her inside and then drove her home, the silence stretching between them like a chasm he didn't know how to cross.

He pulled in the driveway and left the truck running as he went around to open Alexis's door. Insisting he stay this time was the wrong move. And he was done pushing.

He couldn't force anyone to love him. Not Melody, or even his brother, who continued to push him away.

And not Alexis.

As much as he cared about her, she would never reciprocate. It was time to move on. Four years was long enough.

Alexis paused as she reached the front bumper of his truck.

"Why don't you come inside? We should probably talk."

His heart caught in his throat. As much as he had decided he wasn't going to push her anymore, he wasn't ready to actually hear Alexis tell him to leave her alone.

He swallowed thickly and nodded. "Yeah, okay."

He said a desperate prayer as he turned back to shut off the truck before following Alexis inside.

"Thanks for finding me today," she said. "It's… it's been a long time since I had two panic attacks so close together."

Jared angled his body farther toward her on the couch, giving her his full attention. "So that's what it was? A panic attack?" There was something different in his words, though. He was curious but guarded.

She nodded. "Like I said, it's been a while. Almost a year since the last one, I think. Well, before Ty and Addison's party, I guess."

"What happened? What causes them?"

She picked up her drink, holding the mug in front of her like a shield, grounding herself with the solid warmth of the ceramic in her hands. "I wish I knew. It can honestly be anything. At the party? Maybe the dark. Maybe Chase and his dumb face," she said with irritation. "But sometimes, it's completely out of the blue. Last year, I was in the Taco Bravo drive-thru and I just started feeling my chest squeeze and my heart pound."

She squeezed her eyes shut, humiliated to admit that particular episode, since it felt so ridiculous. "There was literally no reason for anything to have triggered it. But it was thirty minutes until I could pull out of their parking lot."

"Oh, Alex." His voice was soft and tender.

She opened her eyes and found his sympathetic gaze on her. "You asked why I was so late with our lunch," she said with a hint of a sardonic smile. "Pretty sure I told you I got a flat tire."

His eyes widened. "I remember that! I was so upset you hadn't called me to help you change it."

She shrugged. "I probably would have, if it had actually been a tire. Today? Probably the parade, combined with our conversation happening in front of everyone, I think."

He shook his head. "I'm so sorry, Alexis. I never should have–"

"It's not your fault, Jared. That's the entire point. It's my problem to deal with. And I've been dealing with it for years."

"But why haven't you ever said anything? I don't understand why you wouldn't tell me. Or Tessa."

"I know you don't. I don't expect you to understand. I came home from the Marines. I am proud of my service. But... the entire experience was stressful."

"I thought you never saw combat?" Jared asked.

She bristled at his words, not because he asked them harshly, but because they echoed the same question she'd been asked by those she'd served with and by the administrators at the VA who had to rubber stamp her requests for treatment. It wasn't an argument she hadn't heard before.

Jared's question had been genuine, though. She knew he wasn't challenging her statement. He just wanted to understand. "Everything from basic training to my role in intelligence…" She shook her head. "It was a lot. I adapted. I handled it while I was there. And I was a good Marine," she said adamantly.

Jared didn't say anything, and she was grateful he waited for her to finish. "But when I came home, it was like my brain couldn't handle the fact that I *wasn't* about to be yelled at at any minute for being too slow or belittled by a male officer who was still upset about women being Marines in the first place. I couldn't even watch TV for a year because of the things I saw on surveillance videos I was translating. I might not have seen a war zone, but my brain sure felt like it was."

"I had no idea," Jared said. "I wish you'd told me."

Alexis shifted on the couch, tucking herself farther into a ball as she pulled her legs under her. "It's not something I'm proud of. I'm a mess, Jared! You saw me today."

All the pent-up frustration at her secret and her disorder rose to the surface and she listed off all the reasons why she kept it to herself, rapid fire. "At any moment, I could be reduced to a helpless ball of chest pain and hyperventilation! I see a therapist once a week, and I'm on a whole cocktail of medication to help my brain realize that I'm not constantly under attack. It's pretty much textbook PTSD."

She took a deep breath, letting the rant sink in for a moment before she continued.

"Why on earth would I tell anyone about that? For one, it's none of their business. It's my problem to deal with, and I don't need anyone else to get tangled up in my 'crazy chick' web. And for another thing... My pride wouldn't take it. It's hard enough that Heath knows and keeps an eye on me all the time when we're on assignments. Thankfully, it seems like working doesn't set me off at all. But if everyone else knew? I'd feel like I was living under a microscope. Everyone walking on eggshells. Looking at me like I was broken."

"You're not broken," Jared said firmly.

"Sure I am. My brain is broken. And it's fine, mostly. The medication helps. My therapist says I'm stable. But look at today. I ruined both of our days, not to mention Trevor's."

"Yeah, let's not mention Trevor," Jared said, his voice letting her know he was unimpressed with her date, which made her smile despite herself.

"I'm just saying... I don't want everyone to know." She stared down at her nearly empty hot chocolate.

She could feel Jared's eyes on her.

"So why did you tell me?" he asked softly.

She glanced up sharply. "What?"

He grabbed the cup from her hands and put it on the table. "Don't get me wrong, I'm incredibly glad you finally shared this piece of yourself with me. I'm just wondering... why me? Why now?"

She shrugged. "I mean... you saw me today. You saw me at the party. I guess I felt like you deserved an explanation." Trying to find the words was difficult. Somehow, she felt like it was time to let him in. She always knew he cared about her, but the last month made it even clearer. "You were so sweet with the Secret Santa gifts. I still can't believe it was you the whole time. I was so sure you wouldn't sign up for it. Every single gift was just... perfect."

Jared studied her, then shifted slightly. He was closer on the couch than she realized. "Is that all it is?"

Alexis swallowed heavily. Nodded. "Yes?" she whispered the answer, a question in itself.

Jared mirrored her nod. "That's why you told me?"

He inched closer, invading her space ever so slowly. Her breath caught in her throat, waiting. Anticipating what was about to happen. "What?" she asked.

"Are you sure that's why you told me? Because I saw you? Because I appreciate the gifts? Or is there more?"

His hand slid across the back of the couch and reached to cradle the side of her neck under her ear. She nearly groaned at the tender contact as she leaned into it.

"Why did you tell me, Alexis?" His raspy question was accompanied by his fingers threading through the hair at the nape of her neck. He must have infinite patience, because the heady silence hung between them for what seemed like an eternity. An impossibly tense and weighty pause, like the crest of a roller coaster just before the huge downhill drop.

"Because I wanted you to see me," she finally admitted, recalling the words from his third note.

At her words, Jared crossed the remaining space. "Oh, sweetheart. I see you. I see all of you."

His lips crashed against hers, and she dropped over the edge of the roller coaster, flying through space in an exhilarating thrill of anticipation finally giving way to the rush of sensation. Tiny explosions of awareness engulfed her as she let herself be carried away on the waves of his kiss.

Softly and sweetly, he murmured her name as she came up for air.

His fingers tangled in her hair as he coaxed her lips with his, drawing her back into the kiss. She pressed forward, aching to feel closer to him. She wanted to feel more. It was as though today's events had unlocked something in her. It had unlocked a willingness to admit what she'd been fighting for so long.

Jared was here.

He'd seen her break. He'd heard her confession.

And he'd stayed.

Just like the secret she'd kept for so long, all the admiration and attraction and joy that she felt around him poured out of the dams she'd tried to contain it in. For once, she embraced the emotions fully, giving up the fight for control and pouring her feelings for him back into the kiss. The ecstasy of his attention covered her completely as he kissed her thoroughly.

Then the intensity subsided, their kiss gentled as he kissed her once, then twice more before pulling back to meet her eyes. His hand still cradled her cheek, and she leaned into it.

Would it be awkward? She waited, holding her breath, unsure of what to say after her entire world had just changed in an instant.

"Where has that been all my life?" he said, his voice full of wonder.

A laugh bubbled up in the back of her throat, then exploded as she tipped her head back in full-fledged joyful laughs. Jared laughed too, and they sat for a moment, sharing in the aftermath of an incredible first kiss that had, if she was honest with herself, been years in the making.

"So," she said, when her laughter had subsided, "what do we do now?" Her head was leaned back on the back of the couch and she stared at the ceiling, a goofy smile still covering her face.

"I'm not exactly sure. But can I vote for doing that again?" Jared's crooked grin greeted her when she looked to her left, where his position mirrored hers.

She grabbed a pillow from behind her and whacked him with it, causing them both to laugh again.

"I'm serious, Jared."

"Hey, so am I! That was… incredible. At least for me," he added.

She heard the touch of insecurity in his voice and she laid her hand on his arm. "Yeah. It was," she agreed. "I'm just… nervous, I guess. We're friends, you know? And I don't want to ruin that."

Jared rolled his neck to the side to look at her instead of the ceiling. "Oh, don't give me that line. That's the most cliche Faithmark line I've ever heard. *We're too good as friends, so we shouldn't be together,*" he mimicked. "That's the biggest copout. That's exactly why we would be great together."

Alexis looked back up. "It's not a copout. It's the truth."

Jared scoffed beside her, and she sat up, pulling his hand into her own after he followed suit.

"Look, all I'm saying is that you're my best friend. And I honestly don't know what I would do if I didn't have you as a friend. Which makes me really nervous to try to be more. Because if something happens and I screw this all up, then where does that leave us?"

Jared shook his head. "There is no way you could screw this up, I promise. If anything, I'm the one with the track record of sending women running for the hills."

She gave him a look. "One woman, Jared. One woman ran for the hills. And from what I hear, you shouldn't beat yourself up about it."

"So what are you saying?"

Alexis took a deep breath. "I don't know. I just…I don't want to rush into anything. Plus, I've got one more stupid blind date to finish." She rolled her eyes. Toby had said New Year's Eve. And she didn't know if he had already set up who it would be, but she couldn't bring herself to care.

She just wanted the blind dates to be over, so she could move forward with Jared. Something about going on a blind date while she was actually dating Jared felt wrong. They could make it two more weeks. "I don't want anything to happen before I have that date."

He frowned. "Why? It's not like it's going to change anything."

She couldn't fault Jared's logic. It wasn't as if she was going to fall in love with this last person, whoever he was.

"It's not that. It's just… It would feel like cheating, you know?"

Maybe after her blind date on New Year's Eve, she could find Jared and have a repeat of that kiss when the clock struck midnight. That sounded like the perfect way to kick off the new year.

15

_J_ared wasn't sure how to respond to Alexis's plea that they not rush. To him, the entire relationship seemed to be moving at a crawl, considering he'd basically been in love with her for at least two of the last four years she'd lived here.

He needed to reassure her that he wasn't going to be scared away by her PTSD. He could handle it. Nothing was insurmountable if it meant being with Alexis. If gradual was what she needed, he'd take things as slowly as she wanted. The important thing was that she knew how he felt. And she felt the same way.

Even if she didn't want to fully admit it yet.

He wasn't going to stop showing her how much he cared, though.

Christmas Eve service with his parents was an important tradition. Much to his excitement, Alexis had agreed to his invitation to join them this year.

At the end of the service, in the candle-lit sanctuary, he said a prayer of thanks for both his parents on one side of him, and Alexis on the other. It felt incredible to have her there with him, finally feeling like they were moving forward in their relationship. Still, he couldn't forget what made Christmas so special. There was nothing better than knowing that Jesus had come into the world and given the gift of salvation. It meant that, despite the brokenness of every person sitting in that church, there was hope.

After the final song, they made their way out of the service and into the lobby, where hot cocoa was being served from the small coffee bar.

After they finished their drinks and his parents left for the night, Jared turned to Alexis. "Do you have some more time tonight? I actually have another gift for you," he said.

She shook her head and her eyes grew wide. "You can't be serious! You already gave me so many things!"

He grinned. "That didn't really count. They were from your Secret Santa."

"Which was you," she countered.

"Oh come on. You'll like it, I promise."

Despite his confidence, he was really hoping

she'd like the gift. He'd been working hard the last week on it, ever since he learned of Alexis's PTSD.

They drove to his place. When they were inside, he flipped on the lamp, instead of the overhead light, keeping the lighting low. His Christmas tree was only about four feet high, but it was lit with white lights and a small scatter of Christmas ornaments.

He directed Alexis to the sofa. "You sit here and let me go get it."

Alexis frowned up at him. "Okay? What is it? You're making me nervous."

"Don't be nervous! Here." He handed her the card he'd written out earlier. "You can read this while I go grab it."

ALEXIS WATCHED with bewildered amusement as Jared rushed out of the living room, leaving her alone in the twinkling Christmas tree glow. Whatever this gift was, he was very excited about it. He shouldn't have gotten her anything. Everything was already too much. Still, she opened the envelope and found the familiar Christmas notecard design he'd used for every Secret Santa gift.

DEAR ALEXIS,

. . .

I KNOW this is an extra gift, but I needed to give you one more thing.

I'll forever be grateful you trusted me with the part of yourself that you've kept hidden. I'm sure I'll mess up sometimes and say the wrong thing, or not come when you call.

I couldn't think of anything better to give you than someone who won't make any of those mistakes.

You don't have to hide your feelings from either of us.

FAITHFULLY YOURS,
Jared and Maverick

AS SHE FINISHED READING the letter, a wet nose nudged her hands and the sweet golden face of Maverick was staring up at her, begging to be petted.

"You're giving me Maverick?" she asked, still trying to understand. Her hands were already cradling the dog's soft face. His tail was wagging excitedly against the sofa.

Jared nodded. "Maverick didn't make the cut for Search and Rescue. But he's the most intuitive dog I've ever worked with. And I've been working with him for the last week on anxiety and stress relief."

She watched, confused, as Jared sat on the floor and tucked his head on his knees. Gently, Maverick came over and nudged his way into the space near Jared's stomach.

"I don't... I don't understand." What was this supposed to be?

Jared stood up. "Together, we'll teach Maverick here what to do when you feel anxious. I've done a bunch of research on it, and people with PTSD say that the dogs really help bring them back before a panic attack is in full swing."

Alexis felt the sting of tears in her eyes. "I can't... I can't accept this. These dogs are crazy expensive." She knew PTSD support dogs were a thing. But she'd never considered getting one herself.

Jared sat on the couch next to her. "Maverick or no Maverick, I'm here to stay. But he needs a good home. And you could use a friend."

Alexis turned and looked up at him. "That's why I've got you, right?"

Jared's cheek lifted. "Always."

She leaned in. Jared's gaze fell to her lips. Everything in her wanted to kiss him. But she held back.

One last blind date stood between them.

"We shouldn't," she whispered. "Not yet."

Jared leaned back, creating space between them that Maverick eagerly filled by jumping on the couch.

"I'm going to egg Toby's truck for this stupid bet," he groaned.

She laughed. "It's almost over. And then we can see where things go, okay?"

Jared ran a hand over his face. "Yeah. Okay. What's one more week, right?"

"Right," she agreed. But as she ran a hand down Maverick's silky golden coat, she wished her hand was running across Jared's beard instead, while his lips teased hers.

"How about some hot cocoa?" Jared offered, interrupting her daydream.

"That sounds good. Movie?"

Jared sighed and looked around. "Yeah okay. Maverick?" He pointed at the dog. "You're the chaperone."

She laughed, but Maverick seemed to take his job seriously. He didn't move from his position between them the rest of the evening. Just before ten o'clock, the movie ended and Jared walked her to the door.

She reached for the doorknob, but turned just before opening. Jared stood close and laid a fist on the doorframe. One arm came forward to wrap around her waist and he pulled her tighter.

Her heartbeat raced at the intensity in his eyes. She tipped her head up, instinctively offering her mouth for a kiss. Jared's eyes fell closed and he groaned. Firmly, he pressed his lips to her forehead. "Merry Christmas, Alexis."

"Merry Christmas," she whispered, surprised at the intensity of her disappointment. She was the one who'd drawn the line in the sand about moving forward before her last blind date. But everything within her wanted to throw that particular conviction out the window into the snowbank.

Maverick let out a small whine, prompting them to pull apart. She immediately missed the feel of Jared's arm around her waist.

"New Year's Eve can't get here fast enough," she said.

"Oh? Looking forward to your date?" Jared said with a wink.

She scoffed. "Yeah right. Looking forward to it being over!"

16

Jared met Toby at Stories and Scones the day after Christmas. It cost him two tickets to the Broncos against the Saints, but Jared convinced him to let Alexis's final blind date be with him.

He sat across from Toby at one of the small tables, his hands wrapped around one of the signature Read. Sip. Repeat mugs that Jan used at the cafe. "Now, don't tell her, okay? I want it to be a surprise."

Toby laughed. "Another surprise? Are you sure you shouldn't just put the girl out of her misery?"

Jared shook his head and grinned. "Nope. Just tell her to be at Evelyn's at seven o'clock, okay?"

Toby raised his eyebrows. "Fancy, fancy," he commented.

Jared shrugged. "It's New Year's Eve, right?"

"Whatever you say, man. She's not going to like it, though."

"You just let me worry about that, okay?"

Toby gave a salute. "You're crazy, man. You really love her, eh?"

Jared nodded. "You have no idea."

Toby's cheerful smile faded and he nodded. "I might have a clue. I hope you get her, mon ami."

"Me too, man. Me too."

They finished their coffee, and Jared headed back to DK9 to take care of the dogs and do some basic training exercises to keep them sharp. Ruby successfully alerted on a stuffed animal that was dusted in one spot with a miniscule amount of peanut powder and Jared hollered in excitement.

"What's the party for?" Alexis's voice came from the corner near the front entrance.

He waved across the training area and jogged her way.

"Did you see that? Ruby's doing amazing with peanut detection."

Alexis smiled. "That's great. When do her new owners come?"

"The second week of January." He glanced back at Ruby, who was wagging her black tail, eagerly waiting for her next task. "She'll be ready."

Alexis climbed over and took a seat on the thick half wall that separated the training area from the offices, her feet dangling off the floor by a foot. Jared leaned on the wall next to her, signaling Ruby to sit at their feet and rewarding her with a treat from the pouch on his waist at her obedience.

Comfortable in the silence between them, he waited for Alexis to speak. It wasn't unusual for her to swing by DK9 unannounced, but he had a feeling today she wasn't just dropping by. A few moments later, she cleared her throat.

"I really don't want to go on this last date," she said.

The corner of his mouth twitched, his heart doing celebratory flips inside his chest. "Oh," he said casually. "Why not?"

She hesitated. "Because I'm ready to date you, goober."

He chuckled at the way she added the light-hearted insult to her confession.

He stood up and turned toward her, stepping between her legs that dangled over the wall. One hand reached for hers, and their fingers laced together. Her seated position meant they were at eye-level, but when he tried to meet her eyes, she was looking down at their joined fingers. He tucked one knuckle under her chin and lifted her face.

"Are you sure you're ready for this?"

She nodded wordlessly.

"Because once we cross this line, we can't go back. You know that, right?"

He inched closer, invading her space. He held his breath, waiting for her to push him away or shake her head to call the entire thing off.

"I'm sure," she whispered.

His lips twitched, itching to kiss her. Instead, he leaned forward, brushing her cheek with his. She tipped her neck to the side, and he nearly gave in to the temptation to press a soft kiss there where her chin and neck met in the intimate spot under her ear. Instead, he whispered, "Good. Then we'll pick this back up after New Year's Eve."

Alexis's hand pulled away from his. She planted both of her hands on his chest and shoved him away. "Ugh, you're a tease, Jared Keen. You know that?"

He laughed as he stepped back. "Me? Four years into this torture and I'm the one to blame?"

"Hey, I didn't know!"

He raised one eyebrow but didn't respond.

Alexis ran a hand through her hair. "Okay, maybe I thought about it. Once or twice."

"That makes two of us," he said with a shrug and a playful smile.

"I can't believe Toby is making me do this. And he said my date wants to go to Evelyn's! Isn't that a bit fancy for a blind date?"

Jared gave a concerned look. "Definitely fancy. Who's the guy?"

She frowned. "I don't know. Toby promised I would have a good time. He said the guy would be there with flowers."

"Yikes." Jared shrugged. "It would probably be cruel to stand him up, right?"

Alexis tipped her head left and right, as though considering the pros and cons. Then she groaned. "I can't do that. Can you imagine how terrible he'd feel? It'll be fine. I'll just meet him for dinner, make a friend, split the bill, and then come find you at the Lodge." The New Year's Eve Party at the Freedom Ridge Lodge was one of the biggest events of the year.

"Are you sure? I could come to Evelyn's. Make a scene and chase him off?" Jared winked to let her know he was joking.

Alexis laughed. "Please don't do that." She hopped off the wall and stepped close, laying a hand on his chest. "Don't be too jealous. I know it's a little strange, but I do need to finish the terms of my bet. And I'm never eating Diablo wings again. Or making a bet with Toby. He's too ornery."

Jared laid his hand on top of hers where it covered his heart. "Good thing I'm not ornery at all."

She narrowed her eyes at him. "Hah. Don't forget I know you better than anyone in town."

He turned his hand, clutching at a pretend arrow in his chest and ripping it out. "Ouch. You wound me."

She laughed, which was his intention. "I think you'll live," she said.

ALEXIS LEFT DK9 FEELING LIGHTER, but it didn't stop the dread she had about her final blind date. She'd tried everything this morning to convince Toby to let her off the hook, but he wouldn't. He said he owed the guy big time and did his best to reassure her that it would be low pressure, no expectations. Just a nice guy who wanted some company for the evening.

Still, she couldn't help but feel guilty as she got dressed for the evening. She was thinking about what Jared was going to think of her navy-blue sequined dress. Imagining him tucking his arm around her waist where the fabric gathered before flowing down to just below her knees. Her date didn't factor into the consideration at all.

The dress was highly impractical for a December night in the mountains, but like every woman, she had accepted that sometimes you just had to accept being cold for the sake of a good party dress.

Though she usually left her face bare of makeup

and her hair tied up, tonight she carefully lined her eyes and dug her ancient eyeshadow palette out of the drawer. She curled her hair and left it long around her shoulders.

She'd get through dinner, and then she could look forward to the rest of the evening with Jared. Assuming Toby hadn't set her up with a serial killer.

She laughed at the thought. Even that wasn't going to stop her tonight, honestly. After years of denying her feelings, hiding her condition, and convincing herself that she was too broken for anyone to love, she would move heaven and earth to be with Jared.

They were on the precipice of an amazing future together, she could feel it. All that stood in their way was a romantic dinner at Evelyn's with someone else.

Maybe she *should* just stand him up. Toby might be upset, but he'd get over it.

She finished applying her mascara and studied herself in the mirror.

No, she wouldn't do that. But maybe if she just showed up to the date and explained the situation, the guy would have pity on her and just let her go.

Or maybe she could send someone in her place? What was Shayla doing tonight?

Her phone dinged with a text message.

Jared: Can't wait to see you tonight. I'm saving a kiss for you at midnight!

A goofy grin spread across her face.

Alexis: Can we fast forward to then?

Jared: Go have your date with the mystery man. Promise you won't fall in love with him and leave me high and dry?

Alexis: No worries there. I promise!

She checked her watch. It was time to go. The sooner she went on the date, the sooner she could leave it.

"Wish me luck, Maverick," she said with a pat on the head for the dog as she headed to the door.

Evelyn's was an upscale restaurant on the corner of Town Square in a huge old Victorian-style house. She parked down the block and walked toward the restaurant, which was still decked out with Christmas lights and garland on the porch.

She stepped inside the warm, cozy interior, searching for her mystery date. A small table caught her eye, a bouquet of flowers resting on the edge. A man was seated at the table with his back to her. He had on a suit coat, but other than that, she couldn't tell who he was in the dim lighting.

With a deep breath, she approached the table, trying to focus on what would come after. She just had to get through dinner.

When she was close to the table, she started her introduction. "Hi, are you waiting for…"

Jared's dark-brown eyes glanced up at her, his broad smile catching her off guard. She looked around. "What are you doing here?"

He stood and came around the table to pull out her chair. What was happening? Did Jared have a date too?

"Relax, Alex. I'm your last blind date."

She shook her head. "No… that can't be right. Toby said…"

"Toby said your date was a nice guy who wanted company for dinner. That's me. Specifically, I want *your* company for dinner."

She laughed, still in disbelief. "You're kidding. How? Toby's so stubborn. How did you get him to agree to this?"

Jared shrugged. "I explained that I hadn't had the opportunity to go on a blind date with you, and that I was clearly a better candidate than Chase or Trevor or Logan. Oh, and I told him that I was in love with you. And I gave him tickets to the Saints game in Denver next month."

She was hanging on every word he said, still amazed that she wasn't sitting here on one last dreadful blind date.

She was here with Jared. And he was in love with her.

"Oh dear. I think that means I broke my promise."

Jared frowned. "What do you mean?"

The corner of her mouth turned up. "I promised you I wouldn't fall in love with my blind date tonight. Too late."

Jared's eyes locked on hers and his mouth fell open. "Really?"

She nodded and leaned forward. "How could I not? I'm sorry I fought it for so long. You're my best friend. You drive me absolutely crazy, but you also make me so incredibly happy. I never thought it was possible."

Jared just shook his head. "You don't have to say it if you're not ready. I don't want to rush you into anything."

"You're not rushing me. You've been so patient. Too patient, probably, but I'm not complaining."

Jared reached for her hand. "I love you so much, Alex. I don't want you to ever doubt that."

"I won't. If the last month has proven anything, it's that you know me better than anyone in the world. I'm still a little scared that a few months from now, you'll decide I'm not worth the trouble."

Jared immediately started shaking his head in denial, but she kept going. "I know that sounds crazy, after everything you've done to show other-wise. You'll just have to keep reminding me, okay?"

He squeezed her fingers. "I'll remind you every day, okay? And if that's not enough, I'll remind you every hour. I'll pray for you and for us, just like I have been since the very beginning."

Tears sprang to her eyes at the intensity of the devotion evident in his voice. She nodded, unable to say anything through the lump in her throat. Jared had pursued her with words and actions and gifts. She'd never felt more treasured or loved.

Their friendship was the perfect foundation on which to build a relationship that would last. Despite her anxieties or the dark shadows that crept in more often than she would like, she knew that Jesus would be there, like He always had been.

And she trusted Jared would be there. He saw all of her and loved her anyway.

And of all the incredible gifts he'd given her this Christmas, that was the very best one.

EPILOGUE

*J*ared slid his arm around Alexis's waist as they wove through the crowded ballroom at Freedom Ridge Lodge. It felt as if the entire town was here, dressed up for the occasion. Upbeat music played, but the sound of cheerful conversations filled the room.

"Well, cher, you look absolutely beautiful." Jared turned toward Alexis to find Toby coming toward the two of them. "And you clean up pretty good too, my man."

Alexis leaned in to give their friend a hug. "I'm not very happy with you, mister!" she said, but the broad smile on her face said otherwise.

Toby grinned. "Just one last surprise, cher! It was his idea," he said, pointing at Jared.

Jared held up his hands in an innocent gesture.

"Hey, don't throw me under the bus. You could have let her off the hook anytime you wanted to."

"Eh. Where's the fun in that?" He winked at them and then hurried across the room to say hello to someone else.

"I suppose we should thank him," Jared said. "The idea of you going on ten blind dates is what made me realize I had better make a move if I was ever going to."

Alexis looked surprised at his confession. "Really?"

He nodded. "That day you lost the bet was the day I decided to try to beg Trudy to make me your Secret Santa."

Alexis laughed. "I didn't know you set that up!"

He shook his head. "I tried to. But Trudy wouldn't go for it. She said God would work it out." He shrugged. "And He did. I got your name in the drawing–my Christmas miracle." He leaned in to kiss her cheek.

"Hey, hey! What was that?" Tessa's animated voice came from his left. "Did I just see… Are you two…?" She gestured between him and Alexis, asking the unspoken question. "Alexis, you have some explaining to do!"

Alexis gave Tessa a hug. "Yes, we're dating. Yes, it's new. Yes, you were right. No, there is no wedding date. Anything else?"

Tessa yelled in excitement. "Ah! This is so exciting." Her eyes went wide and she gasped, turning toward him. "You were the Secret Santa!"

He nodded. "Guilty as charged."

Tessa's eyes softened and she smacked Alexis on the shoulder. "And there is no wedding date yet? Are you crazy?"

"Slow down, tiger. We're taking it slow."

"Not too slow, I hope!" Tessa countered. Jared stifled a laugh, and she turned back to him. "You be good to her, you hear?"

He nodded. "I will."

"And don't let her sabotage it, okay?"

"I'm standing right here, you know," Alexis said with a laugh.

"I'm just saying. It's about time you two figured out that you were perfect for each other. Don't mess it up." Tessa pointed her finger at both of them.

"I love you, Tessa," Alexis said, hugging her friend again. "Now go bug Adam or something."

Tessa laughed but shuffled away to track down her husband in the crowd.

Jared put his hand back around Alexis's waist, pulling her closer and kissing the side of her temple.

Tessa wasn't the only one to react to their new relationship status with joy and "it's about time" sentiments. But Jared couldn't imagine anything he'd rather do than be surrounded by the friends and community of Freedom with Alexis by his side.

Just before midnight, Haven Gilbert took the microphone and thanked everyone for coming to the event. She led the countdown and the crowd cheered, "Happy New Year!" together.

Jared pulled Alexis into his arm and tucked one hand around the nape of her neck. "Happy New Year, my love."

She smiled and lifted to her tiptoes. Jared tightened his hold on her waist and pressed his lips against hers in an overwhelming celebration of not only the promise of a new year ahead, but of the relationship they were finally embarking on together.

"I love you so much," she whispered when their kiss ended.

A smile teased his lips. "You have no idea how long I've waited to hear you say that."

"I love you. I love you."

He captured her mouth with his again, unable to do anything else while he was filled with emotion at her words. He hadn't been sure it would really happen. Secret Santa opportunity or not, he knew how much had to be overcome in the last month to get to this place. He could be honest about the strength of his feelings, and Alexis could be vulnerable about the challenges she faced every day.

He pulled back, leaning his forehead against hers as he caught his breath.

"What's wrong," she asked.

He shook his head slightly. "I'm just so happy to be here with you, sweetheart. I keep thinking I'm going to wake up from a dream any second."

Alexis gave a mischievous smile. "You want me to pinch you?"

He smirked, enjoying the fact that a shift in their relationship was only going to enhance the jokes and banter they shared. It would be like continuing to be best friends with Alexis, but deeper.

Loving her held the same steady warmth of their friendship. But now, instead of a soft glow, it was an intense fire that consumed everything within him. He'd never be the same.

He could be unapologetically himself with her. The same powerful, open-handed love he offered that had scared one woman away was exactly what Alexis needed to be reassured it was real.

He kissed her again, loving the freedom to do exactly what he'd imagined a hundred times. "No pinching necessary. Happy New Year, Alexis."

ACKNOWLEDGMENTS

When God called me to step out in faith and start a collaborative series, I had no idea what He would accomplish through it. So first and foremost – Father, I am so unbelievably grateful for opportunities you have given me. For this book and all the others – but especially the friends I have made while walking in (sometimes reluctant) obedience.

Those friends include the amazing Mandi Blake and Hannah Jo Abbott. I wouldn't be who I am as a writer, mother, or woman without you! I thank the Lord for you every day.

This series could not have been what it is without the other authors as well – Liwen Ho, Elle E. Kay, and Jessie Gussman; thank you for jumping on board this crazy vision and making it a thousand times more than I ever expected. Thanks for being wonderful human beings to work with.

Writing Jared and Alexis's story was really fun. After writing two romantic suspense books this year, I was determined to write a Christmas book full of light-hearted holiday cheer! But I love that light-hearted stories can still hit tough topics. Alexis's struggle with PTSD and the related anxiety and depression was important for me to write. I did my best to write her experience as authentically as I could, but I know every person's experience is different.

Thank you to Brandi from Editing Done Write for fixing a million misplaced commas and making sure my Secret Santas were consistent!

Lastly, thank you to my amazing husband. You are endlessly patient, accommodating, and encouraging as I pursue this crazy dream. I love doing life with you and you are, without a doubt, my favorite human.

Mister B, Little C, and Baby L… Mama loves you beyond words.

Heroes of Freedom Ridge Series

(Year 1)
Rescued by the Hero (Aiden and Joanna)
Mandi Blake
Love Pact with the Hero (Jeremiah and Haven)
Liwen Y. Ho

(Year 2)
Healing the Hero (Daniel and Ashley)
Elle E. Kay
Stranded with the Hero (Carson and Nicole)
Hannah Jo Abbott

(Year 3)
Reunited with the Hero (Max and Thea)
M.E. Weyerbacher
Forgiven by the Hero (Derek and Megan)
Tara Grace Ericson

(Year 4)
Guarded by the Hero (Heath and Claire)
Mandi Blake
Trusting the Hero (Ty and Addison)
Hannah Jo Abbott

(Year 5)

Believing the Hero (Pete and Jan)
Tara Grace Ericson
Friends with the Hero (Tuck and Patience)
Jessie Gussman

(Year 6)
Persuaded by the Hero (Bryce and Sabrina)
Elle E. Kay
Romanced by the Hero (Mac and Amy)
Liwen Y. Ho

(Year 7)
Faith in the Hero (Chris and Gretchen)
Jessie Gussman
Second Chance with the Hero (Jack and Josephine)
Liwen Ho

(Year 8)
Inspired by the Hero (Gage and Casey)
Elle E. Kay
Hope for the Hero (Adam and Tessa)
Mandi Blake

(Year 9)
Running to the Hero (Jude and Felicity)
Hannah Jo Abbott
Blind Date with the Hero (Jared and Alexis)
Tara Grace Ericson

BOOKS BY TARA GRACE ERICSON

Black Tower Security Series - (Romantic Suspense)

Potential Threat

Hostile Intent

Critical Witness

Second Chance Fire Station

The One Who Got Away

The One She Can't Forget

The Main Street Minden Series

Falling on Main Street

Winter Wishes

Spring Fever

Summer to Remember

Kissing in the Kitchen: A Main Street Minden Novella

The Bloom Sisters Series

Hoping for Hawthorne - A Bloom Family Novella

A Date for Daisy

Poppy's Proposal

Lavender and Lace

Longing for Lily

Resisting Rose

Dancing with Dandelion

Heroes of Freedom Ridge (multi-author series)

Forgiven by the Hero

Believing the Hero

ABOUT THE AUTHOR

Tara Grace Ericson lives in Missouri with her husband and three sons. She studied engineering and worked as an engineer for many years before embracing her creative side to become a full-time author. Now, she spends her days chasing her boys and writing books when she can.

She loves cooking, crocheting, and reading books by the dozen. Tara unashamedly watches Hallmark movies all winter long, even though they are predictable and cheesy. She loves a good "happily ever after" with an engaging love story. That's why Tara focuses on writing clean contemporary romance, with an emphasis on Christian faith and living. She wants to encourage her readers with stories of men and women who live out their faith in tough situations.

Made in the USA
Monee, IL
13 November 2023

46429721R00121